T0021349

Karolinum Press

MODERN SLOVAK CLASSICS

Ján Johanides
But Crime
Does Punish

Translated from the Slovak
by Julia and Peter Sherwood

Afterword by Robert B. Pynsent

KAROLINUM PRESS 2022

KAROLINUM PRESS
Karolinum Press is a publishing department
of Charles University
Ovocný trh 560/5, 116 36 Prague 1
Czech Republic
www.karolinum.cz

This book has received a subsidy from SLOLIA Committee,
the Centre for Information on Literature in Bratislava, Slovakia.

LITERÁRNE
INFORMAČNÉ
CENTRUM

Cover and graphic design by Zdeněk Ziegler
Set and printed in the Czech Republic by Karolinum Press
First English edition

Cataloging-in Publication Data is available
from the National Library of the Czech Republic

ISBN 978-80-246-5014-2 (pbk)
ISBN 978-80-246-5128-6 (pdf)
ISBN 978-80-246-5129-3 (epub)
ISBN 978-80-246-5130-9 (mobi)

All my life I have been saying, obligingly: May I? May I? May I? - the way you do when you try to fight your way down the crowded corridor of an express train, but people heading in the opposite direction have always politely pushed me back, back to the place where I uttered my first "May I?" And that is why I'm laughing now.

It was here, in this castle, in this last refuge - that is, in this *donjon*, or somewhere around here, in the middle of this oriel to be precise, before these three windows, the tallest in the castle, perhaps in precisely the same spot where you and I are sitting now - that the chatelain of the royal castle would spend many a night, keeping vigil.

Sometimes, mostly in the autumn and usually late at night, when I open the window to clear cigarette smoke and my poetry from the room, which by this time of the morning tends to have become even more stale than usual, I sense the chatelain's presence. Not that I hear floorboards creaking or door handles turning, no: I am no advocate of ghosts. I simply sense the chatelain's presence - and by that I don't mean his personal presence, but rather something from four centuries ago. As if someone's presence has continued to linger here, in this oriel window. Someone who has stayed up all night in this place, someone who has been complicit - while at the same time keeping his distance from his own complicity - and for this reason his confusion could not betray anyone. For I have a confession to make: there is precious little in this world that I relish more than maintaining a certain distance from what I am experiencing at this very moment, from what at this very moment I am obliged to experience.

So you'd say this is more of a small goblet than a glass, would you? Don't be deceived by appearances: it is just the thickness of the glass that makes it seem like that. Good old glass. – That glass over there, the one filled with red wine, is also just an ordinary glass, just like the ones you and I are drinking from and which you have called goblets. – Your health. – So let me say it again: welcome to my home. You're right: this kirsch is truly superb. Mind you, that's something I deserve credit for. We are fortunate enough to have a first-rate distillery in the neighbourhood. A renowned distillery. Its manager is rather aged, but he is a genius of a man, a legend of a man, someone who still knows "who" the distilled spirit is rather than "what" it is. Except that in his case one swallow really does make a summer: that's what makes our distillery peerless. Some people – and our distiller is an example – have a capacity for emotion that goes well beyond the lack of sensitivity typical of the majority who make do with sensations, presenting them as emotions. So, you think that I am first and foremost my own spectator. So be it. To your health, once more. By the way – has my dog given a paw to you yet? Regent, have you given a paw to our visitor? Come here, give a paw to our visitor, there's a good boy! – Hm. He won't: that's rather unusual. Normally it's the other way round. He often goes out of his way to give a paw. The only people he won't give a paw to are those he has taken a dislike to, or who are at death's door. Don't take it personally.

Do you detect... do you really think that you detect a look of despair in Regent's eyes? – Why? – Do you see in them a kind of pleading helplessness? – Can you read dogs' eyes? – What about their bodies? – He has tautened the odd muscle, his hair is bristling here and there, he seems to be ready to jump, and now – can you hear the sudden barking sounds he is making? While his watchful eyes are beginning to express something impossible to put into words – and if it *were* possible, it would be too dodgy. That means imprecise. He'd let you see his face and then you could try to decipher it, one syllable at a time. It may simply puzzle you if you don't like dogs. Do you see? My Regent has now turned to me, as if wanting to utter some stern reproof. His resonant, yet hoarse, voice, sounds belligerent more than anything else. Though I admit that it also conveys some fear that is hard to define. This coarse, aggressive fear that springs from his dog's throat that never stopped moving during that first deafening barrage of barking, reminiscent of a deep, full-bloodied cough. In that rasping bark of his there is a kind of distrust as if, at this very moment, the dog were making the utmost effort to reprimand his master or, at least, to articulate by this hoarse yelping how his master should behave.

You can see it yourself: my dog has taken a dislike to you, but that doesn't mean we shouldn't continue this conversation.

It is odd, to say the least: now my dog seems to have taken against you, and earlier today there was this woman. A woman who came to warn me about you indirectly.

Just imagine, at about a quarter past seven this morning, a completely strange woman turns up here, claiming she has been sent by our mutual friend. That would, of course, be none other than our dear pharmacist Mr Hubert Vrtiak. She said he'd asked her to tell me that we – that is, you, Mr Klementini, and I – should postpone our meeting for the time being. I asked her why. She replied, somewhat brusquely, that all she had been told was to pass on this message to me, and after a moment's pause she added that Mr Vrtiak was sure to provide me with a detailed explanation in person. I asked her, probably equally curtly, about the nature of her relationship to Mr Vrtiak: was she a relation of his and why didn't he send her with a note to give me. She replied that she was a good friend of his (I am familiar with the floral type of Vrtiak's lady friends – but she was not one of that kind). I remarked that I would verify the message at once, and immediately rang the pharmacist, on the quite erroneous assumption that I would not find him at the pharmacy precisely on account of this matter. Surprisingly enough, he was there, but all he had to say was what I have told you a moment ago. I remember telling him: But you were insisting that Klementini should come and see me at lunchtime today, and now you've gone and turned everything upside down. Why? At least explain to me briefly what this is all about. Only yesterday, and the day before, you rang to confirm our appointment. He said that he – that is you, Mr Klementini – knew best how much he had done for you so that you'd be obliged to agree to a postponement. I really don't know what service Vrtiak might have done you – he is not exactly one to squander good deeds – but don't worry, I'm not Vrtiak's guard dog. The pharmacist wanted me to give you a ring as soon as possible and cancel your visit. And did I ring you? No, I didn't. So there you have it! You're sitting here, so there's no problem. Or is there? No, everything's fine.

I don't like secretiveness, Mr Klementini. Don't you dare leave now! Yes, that's an order. And an order's an order. You heard me right. I mean it. Don't do anything you might come to regret. Let's have a drop more kirsch instead. Believe me, I couldn't care less about Vrtiak's request that we postpone our meeting – I thought it was just one of his whims, something one can blame on his astrological calculations. Actually, this message, this information, wouldn't have surprised me at all had it not been conveyed by that incredible woman. If he had just rung me about it himself. No need to be alarmed, I'm sure Regent will gladly give you a paw of his own accord, it just seems to me it's that incredible woman who has given rise to Regent's mistrust. It's rare for this kind of thing to happen to me – it wasn't the message that upset me, as I said, but the woman's appearance. Vrtiak has been known to change his plans on the basis of the horoscopes, which he draws up for you, for me or for himself (as he does from time to time for the following day), even when he had sworn to keep his word. No, what stressed me out was the way that woman looked and behaved.

After the horrifying ringing of the doorbell, I went to open the door.

The first thing that struck me about this woman, above all else, were her enormous, bulging eyes, their whites as white as black people's, as bone china, whites without any visible blood vessels (I wonder if she uses eyedrops), the dark irises melding into the pupils and reflecting the morning light in a way reminiscent of the gleaming black of overripe dark red cherries at dusk. I saw motionless eyes without any make-up. And I felt that they issued some sort of challenge, desire but also, at the same time, a command, that seemed to be driven by some pertinacity, urgency, a doggedness of the kind high fever sometimes lends one's eyes. This unfamiliar woman's face seemed as bloodless as if it had paled after reading a so-called fateful telegram. She had yet to utter a word.

There was no doubt that it was she who had rung the bell, she was the only one who could have done so, taking a tentative step forward, then stopping and retreating, indeed jumping back from the door. But why? At that moment she seemed to have only just started to approach the door and was about to reach for the doorbell. She rang it in the kind of impatient and peremptory manner you might expect of an ambulance driver, the criminal police or an irate neighbour. I walked towards her. In this young woman there was something of the frailty of a bouquet of dried, fragile blossoms, a posy of immortelles, those unfading, deciduous flowers sold for the winter season. No doubt, in her own way, an uncommonly pretty woman (although beside the striking gold around her neck, a refined eye would immediately discern in the unfamiliar woman's complexion the first signs of ageing, even if the delicate wrinkles on her skin would have been unlikely to attract anyone's attention had she not been wearing jewellery). This woman in a simple dress the colour of a sparrow's breast who stood there in the morning in the doorway, her arms held out before her – as if holding some bulky object that she was about to hand me – had striking fingers and palms: they looked exactly as if the salty flesh of dissected sea fish had been corroding them day in, day out. She can't possibly be working in a canning factory, I thought, staring at her blotchy knuckles. Did she deliberately avoid using hand cream? Or medicated cosmetics? Was she not seeing a dermatologist? Was she handling chemicals without gloves? Deliberately? Perhaps intentionally? She displayed her hands as if flaunting misfortune of some kind. She certainly gave the impression of someone intent on playing cards with her own wounds as if they were jokers. Why couldn't she relax? Why didn't she shake hands, although she had clearly intended to (at least, to judge by the movement she made). Eczema on her hands? Who was this strange woman? And anyway: if she and the pharmacist were such good friends, why did he let her go around with hands like that? What was it she wanted? Who had she come to see? Why didn't she speak? What was she really after? Why wouldn't she lower those hands of hers? She rang five or six times and by the time I finally got up and went out into the hallway, she was silent and just stood there panting. Was she asthmatic? Had she suddenly lost the faculty of speech? Had she got cramp? A fright? Whom did she seek? Was it me? Why hadn't she uttered a single word yet? Was she looking for a member of staff? Someone from the permanent display of flora and fauna?

Only when I examined her from head to toe, during that anxious moment filled with the loud breath escaping into the silence out of her thin lips, only then was I able to take in the details of her eyes, nose, cheeks, mouth, eyebrows, chin, and temples, and realized that the wholly girl-like face of this woman going on forty had been gradually, roughly moulded by long years of cares, that the way she responded to countless stimuli had been driven by justified fear, that it was her ability to stay as alert as a policeman or a devious murderer that had trained her to exercise caution, which she used as something like traffic-lights. I sensed that, despite the gold around her neck, this unpigeonholeable woman had lived a black-and-white existence, stripped-down and monotonous, over a vast, grey period during which the only green that she saw was a few tired, dusty trees surrounded by the concrete of a prison courtyard, that she had been eking out an existence outside the maelstrom of our society, at home as in some sort of abroad, behind bars, that she had long become estranged from people, that she had grown apart from them and turned into a raven, that she was the embodiment of loneliness, flying under heavy night clouds, that she really was a raven woman, which might explain why her face seemed so unnatural and so delicate, as if her spirit were leaning out of her real face: I felt that if I blew on her with the full force of my lungs, she might shatter before my very eyes like the fluffy globe of a dandelion.

In that unusual, uncertain moment pregnant with questions, I noticed that further down the staircase below this strange woman, someone was waiting. No doubt waiting for her.

It was only then that she uttered her first words. After a silence lasting at least three minutes. Then, having waited for me to make the phone call to Vrtiak, she immediately turned to leave; I think without saying goodbye.

That woman was really unusual, though what she said wasn't actually an explicit warning about you – I don't know why I put it like that earlier, a slip of the tongue and before you know it, a long explanation is necessary, it happens to us all – so how about some red wine? Red wine suggests – for me at least – a kind of reassurance. There is something mysterious about it, its bitter notes often force us to probe ourselves thoroughly from within to ensure that we haven't yet disappeared. Yes, that's right, my dear sir. Sometimes the taste of red wine, combined with the rich aroma of dried wild mushrooms and the charred smell of freshly chopped logs from fir trees can give rise to a yearning for Christmas even in high summer. But you should start by sampling these milk-caps – they're a speciality of mine. Kirsch followed by milk-caps, and then we'll have a taste of this smoked pike. You won't regret it. And to go with it, a drop of Müller

Thurgau – the perfect accompaniment to smoked fish. Vrtiak said you were a great gourmet. Don't worry, just relax. None of this is of any consequence. Well, what do you think – I wasn't misleading you, was I? A tart, tangy and velvety bouquet – yes, that's it, exactly. What do you mean? That's a term I don't apply to gastronomy, ever. I'm sorry, I didn't catch what you said. I admit I might have called our meeting off, had that woman not looked the way she did. If it hadn't been for the way she looked, I'd have called it off. She was so peculiar that even if she'd taken an ordinary box of matches out of her handbag, I would have had my suspicions about the box. No, I don't believe in that sort of thing. Fate. Do you believe in fate? I don't. When I hear people say that fate had driven someone to do something, I... – But there's one thing I know for sure: if you come up against something mindboggling, you have found yourself at the point where, as people say, the outskirts of God begin, though not quite on the street that leads directly to Him.

I gather from how you have turned up here and, in particular, from what brought you here, that you have come expecting an experience of the utmost importance. That's what Vrtiak said, too, he said that for you this might be the most important thing of all. The most important thing in your life. This is how people make preparations for suicide, a wedding, their mother's funeral. Please don't make that face, like a wet dog that wants to rub itself on my leg. I can see you have a sense of humour. Now, let's get to the point:

Everyone has something they call their most significant memory. The most significant of all the significant ones. A memory that will never fade, come what may. Or a memory that can't be washed off like old blood stains.

The most significant memory always comes back to us unexpectedly. It startles us every now and then like the shrill ringing of an alarm clock that we didn't set, suddenly taking us aback, making us wonder why it is ringing and why now, of all times. You know the feeling, don't you? It's like a burn that healed a long time ago and is now warning you of an impending frost. How odd: why is the memory that has taken the deepest root inside us never a happy one?

So let me get to the point:

When I turned twenty-two, to be more precise I was twenty-two plus a few hours, a large gathering took place at our house. Among those who turned up – or rather, who suddenly remembered my existence – were not only my friends from the printing works, my old schoolfriends, girls from the grammar school and a few close relations, but also some distant relations, the kind of extended family we can only describe as the scattered litter of some elderly sow.

Laughter, hoary anecdotes, humour patched together out of well-worn jokes, people talking about this and that. I forget what brought it on, but I remember distinctly that, all of a sudden, everyone in my family, from the closest relations to the most distant kin I had never seen before, was hell-bent on holding forth. It was a kind of boasting contest – don't get me wrong, Mr Klementini, I'm not saying there wasn't some truth to all their bragging. Absolutely not. Every single one of them, as I learned later, was telling his own truth, except that each of them squeezed it into a frame that was as tawdry as it was ostentatious, and they would all have sounded quite plausible if they hadn't been drunk, if they hadn't been flailing their arms around, if they hadn't put on such airs and graces, if they hadn't sworn blind, hands on hearts, that they were telling the truth, and if they hadn't stroked their knees as if they belonged to the grammar-school girls sitting across the room. The only one who didn't say a word was my grandfather.

They got into almighty rows, of course, about all kinds of things. And of course, it was inevitable that each of them talked mainly about things they had experienced themselves.

I don't really remember, try as I might, how the idea came up that everyone should share the most powerful experience of their lives. Everyone clapped. And then, without further ado, someone announced – even standing up to make the announcement – that his most unforgettable experience was something that happened when he was doing his military service as a border guard near Mikulov, something that, at a stroke, had propelled him from a stripeless soldier to a corporal. And the reason it happened was that he had fired his machine gun, preventing someone from crossing the border from Czechoslovakia into Austria. With his cheeks bright red, like a TB sufferer in his death throes, he told us, all flushed, how dark that night had been. His story went something like this:

"... I tore right through him with that shot. I tore a jagged line through the man. Like a blunt pair of scissors cutting a sheet of metal. Later I saw him being dragged away. And I was promoted to corporal on the spot. I was number one in my regiment! I wish you'd seen it! You wouldn't believe where they sat me in the canteen and who I shared the table with! After midnight the colonel... (now he was stammering, overcome with emotion) said that I should read Boris Polevoy's *The Story of a Real Man,* as I was the only real man in the ranks, all the others were only good for target practice – they were so scared!

But the most important thing was that I was granted home leave straight away! Four days later I was on my way home, and as a corporal to boot! I even had time to have my trousers taken in. By seven o'clock I was in bed with my Marka!" he said, still amazed, and continued: "Just ask Marka, she'll confirm it. You will confirm it, Marka, won't you? And we weren't sleeping in her house! We were at my mum's! She made our bed and turned the heating on in the front room. She put one duvet underneath us and another, thinner one, on top and said: 'Enjoy yourselves, children, enjoy yourselves!' I'll never forget that as long as I live! I won't forget the way my mum said it either (he giggled), or how I tore right through that man with my volley, or how I got promoted, or how I sat across the table from the commander of our regiment, everyone around me a major – all in all, this was the most wonderful thing that ever happened to me!"

All this time my grandfather sat there without saying a word. Then, all of a sudden, he started to speak, after gesturing for silence. He said: "Now I have a story to tell you, a story I'm never going to forget either. You all know that I'm nearly eighty, don't you?" Then he proceeded to tell us how he'd fought in the Great War, having been called up back in 1914, sent first to Bosnia, then ending up on the Eastern Front by 1915. He told us how in late October a "sliver of shrapnel" had lodged in his right hand, and since his middle finger "didn't heal properly", he was retrained as a stretcher bearer. He went on to tell us about the Russian army facing the Austrians, and about the Austrian Poles who were roped in as interpreters for captive Russians, while all this time he had "kept mum" about the fact that he was also fluent in Russian, having spent twelve years in Petrograd working at the Országh department store as deputy head of haberdashery, adding that back then, in 1915, you could keep "a whole lot of things" secret, even after being called up. He said that no one, neither his commanding officer, the colonel, nor the padre was aware that he could speak Russian. Then he told us about the hundreds of Orthodox believers who served in his regiment. Not all of them were pure-blooded Serbs though. They were a motley bunch, mainly lads from near the Serbian borders – young men from the Voivodina as well as Dalmatia, specially deployed by the K. und K. army high command to the north and to the Eastern Front, so that "they wouldn't end up bayonet-charging Serbs, you know, men who spoke the same language and were of the same faith." Grandfather then told us about his second Christmas in the trenches. This, he noted, was no longer a jingoistic Christmas: this time there was no swagger, nobody shouting „Long live the war!" as they had the year before, and then he pointed out it was time to get to the crux of the matter:

"In the year one thousand nine hundred and fourteen as well as fifteen – and also earlier, of course – Christmas was taken very seriously indeed, dead seriously. On the Front, too, it was regarded as the day of the birth of the Son of God. All fighting stopped – not a shot was fired, neither side attacked the other – it was an unwritten law – at least on the Eastern Front. You could safely stick your head above the parapet. Neither side had announced an armistice in advance. But on Christmas Eve everything went so quiet that you could hear sparrows landing on the bird-cherry trees. The main thing I want to say, the thing that I really want to say above all, is that the Russians didn't fire or launch any attacks on Christmas Eve, or on Christmas Day, or on St Stephen's Day, and that we, I mean all of us on the Austrian side, launched no offensives during their Orthodox Christmas either. But then this happened: somehow – I still have now idea how – one of the men must have got wind that I had worked in Russia, in Petrograd, and that made them wonder if I had at least some Russian. So they come over to me, take me to one side, into a corner, a fork in the trenches – I was already an officer by then – and without beating about the bush they come up with the idea that I should take them over to the Russian trenches so that they could celebrate the birth of the Son of God in their own way. Believe me, my first thought was that they might be Russian spies, but I dismissed that idea straight away – they were burly, semi-literate chaps with hands like millstones, driven to distraction by all the fighting, peasants from Novi Sad or further south – some other far-flung corner, in short. I admit that the idea of defecting to the Russians had indeed crossed my mind – I had met this woman in Petrograd and had thought of proposing to her – I just didn't know how to go about it and was waiting for some God-given opportunity, since we medics didn't have a chance of surrendering to the Russians in the thick of battle, where bellies were being slit open. So I promised these Orthodox lads that I would take them across – because I was scared for myself, or scared of them – even though I couldn't be sure that I'd be able to keep my word.

But there's no putting off holidays and time flies by. At some point I felt that the right moment had arrived. Our company commander had just received a letter from home. He got sozzled and was blubbing like a baby as I put him to bed. And so, come evening, we crawled across the blasted land, that zig-zagging strip of earth. There was a beautiful sunset. It felt strange to be slithering along like slugs in their slime.

We must have been spotted by guards on both sides. The Austrians on our side, as well as the Russians on the other. But none of them pointed their guns at us. Their eyes seemed, how should I put it, to be in on some secret ... or rather, stripped bare like a grocer's that has been turned upside down. Inside out. We're crawling Indian-file, I whispered to one of my companions but, as I discovered later, none of this lot from the Drava region knew what I was talking about. Eventually – by crawling across that blasted strip of land, blessedly serene and drenched like earthworms in some kind of a race – we finally reached the Russian trenches. Tiny Christmas trees decorated with bunting rose on both sides. None of the Russian soldiers – including the low-ranking officers who outnumbered us – was in the slightest surprised to see us! Had they been expecting us? I have no idea. Probably not, but why then were they not taken aback at all? They received us very warmly, and to my great astonishment, shock even, they didn't ask any questions about anything military. I swear this is true. Strange, isn't it? Very strange, to be sure. The only thing we talked about was the birth of Christ. I forgot to mention that my men had brought along a few modest gifts for the Russians – a bit of gingerbread, an apple, a piece of poppyseed cake. Never since have I seen people as happy to be together as these Russians and our Austrian Serbs. They all shed tears, weeping so copiously that their faces looked as if they'd just been pulled out of the water. Pictures emerged from pockets and they showed each other photos of their loved ones. But that was just the beginning. They went on to pray together. They asked why I didn't join in their prayers... I explained that although I could speak Russian, I was a Protestant. They didn't understand. Then they hugged each other again, crossed themselves, exchanged tiny crosses, miniature icons on bits of string around their necks, and then we crept back to the Austro-Hungarian trenches, as quiet as church mice. The rations the Tsar's soldiers received were far less generous than ours, they had no tobacco for example, yet our men showed me the gifts the Russians gave them: a handful of walnuts, a few prunes, and *pirozhki* that had gone hard on their long journey.

But eventually the echo of Catholic Christmas faded away, Orthodox Christmas came and went, the artillery barrage resumed, and the commanding officers launched a bayonet charge, ripping open the bellies, bowels, spleen and chests of soldiers on both sides who shared their faith and whom they had embraced only a week earlier. All of them. Why? By command? Were they following orders? To be sure, they were obeying a command, following an order: it was fear of being killed that forced them to kill. But all that was just the trimmings – in reality it wasn't the command or following orders that mattered; the real reason has always been and will remain a far greater mystery.

I hunkered down in the trenches, ready with my stretcher and all the other paraphernalia, and when the attack was over I watched in horror as one of the men with whom I had crawled over to the Russian side wound a Russian's bowels nimbly and deftly around his bayonet, taking special care to cover the length of the blade."

Can you explain the nature of human beings to me, Mr Klementini? None of us knows ourselves sufficiently well to be able to predict what effect the force of this or that action might have on us. That's why after an experience like that we behave quite differently from the way we might expect. We surprise ourselves. We are caught off-guard by our own actions. We might betray ourselves. For in most people the expanses of the subconscious are even less reliable than ever-shifting sands.

To cut a long story short: I know that Mr Vrtiak, Hubert that is – I assume you're also on first-name terms with him – has already told you a great deal about me. The two of us go back a long way, more than forty years. That's right. I'm sure he has told you all sorts of things about me. He likes to talk about other people, though he never speaks ill of anyone. I don't know if you've noticed – have you known him for long? – that his hearing is phenomenal! He has perfect pitch not just for music, but also for the voices of everyone he knows. You may have had just a single glass of wine and he will know from your voice. You might phone him for one reason or another and the first thing he'll say is: Ondro, have you gone and had a glass of wine without waiting for me? And he'll give a laugh. He would be great in music hall. One thing I can't understand is why he hasn't become a musician. I'm convinced he would have enjoyed worldwide success as a pianist. His playing is wonderful – though I'm no great expert on music. I once asked him how it was possible that he came into this world with such incredibly perfect pitch. He laughed and said that it was probably because his mother, when she was expecting him, was pained by everything beautiful, she had felt great compassion for everything that was beautiful. Was it because of its fleeting nature?

Can you feel compassion for something solely because it is beautiful yet ephemeral? But as I know Vrtiak, he will never offer more than just basic information. No more than an outline. The rest you have to work out for yourself. I'm sure you've also noticed this about him.

So perhaps Vrtiak has also told you that he and I were born under the same sign, in the year of the dragon according to the Chinese and Tibetan calendar. Although he's twelve years younger than me. However, to put it in a way women in this country take more seriously, I was born under the sign of Scorpio, while he is a Gemini. Every now and then, once in a blue moon, he will get it into his head, or someone will ask him, to draw up a horoscope, and then he takes out all his big fat astrological tomes and gets calculating – but none of this really matters. I suppose what does matter is that you can really trust Vrtiak. Which is why I don't understand why he wanted our appointment to be cancelled. Horoscopes are about the only thing that might explain it.

I first met Vrtiak at no. 13, Taškentská Street. In an enormous villa built in the final years of interwar Czechoslovakia. During the Czechoslovak First Republic. We were both renting rooms in the house but were not aware of each other. We'd never met until that moment. Neither in the house nor out in the street. The couple who owned the house were smart business types, but they were unusually considerate landlords nonetheless, very amenable. They even rented out rooms in their cellar. Every wall was whitewashed. A stove in every room. An affable, obliging attitude. A phone line. Cookers. Metal bunk beds. Discretion. Had a female visitor – or not, for that matter? – No one would recall anything. They both worked for the secret police. To cut a long story short: one day – whether it was spring or autumn I forget – I went up to the attic to hang up some vests and underpants to dry. There were always mountains of underwear up there, but this time, out of the blue, I spotted a pair of men's legs, a pair of large men's shoes, size 44 at least, socks and trousers of an indeterminate colour. Swinging in the air, both of them.

A pair of shiny black shoes, the kind once known as brothel creepers that are no longer in fashion: with rounded toe caps and thick soles. And although I could clearly see the shoes, the ankles in the socks and the slightly too-short trousers above them, my unconscious, automatic reaction, without the slightest hesitation, was to refuse to believe that a pair of legs ending in black shoes could possibly be dangling there, just a couple of metres in front of me. I refused to believe my own eyes: that's something you learn inside. I looked away. The reflex that my head had cultivated for years was still in perfect working order. It immediately convinced me that what I was seeing was just some suspended bits of fabric; that it was only the wind blowing above the asbestos cement roof in the dusk, the angle of light in the attic and my own exhaustion, the exhaustion of someone who had been on his feet since two-thirty in the morning – combined with the permanent state of depression that spawns nightmares – that conspired to create the impression that I was seeing a pair of shoes dangling in the air. You see, in order to survive prison, solitary, the catacombs of Valdice – believe me, you have to teach yourself to deny what's right in front of your nose. I had to teach myself – a training I underwent against my will –

to deceive every one of my own senses! But at the same time, I had to become aware that my real eyes needed to beget a pair of fake eyes, because without this pair of fake eyes the real ones wouldn't have survived. You needed elastic lies wherever you were. Including in your own company, of course. In those days I kept forcing myself to believe something that was a sheer impossibility, for without believing in what was impossible I would have had no choice but to use every last bit of my strength to bang my head, regularly and deliberately – like a piledriver ramming piers into a riverbed to build a temporary bridge – against those centuries old, utterly innocent walls.

Except that, once I had trained myself to revel in mirages, to hope that this, that, or the other might be possible after all, I couldn't kick the habit. I wasn't able to rid myself of this scar, this physical defect that had corroded my soul: I had taught myself to see only what I wanted to see and this shadow, which I had myself created under the pressure of Valdice, had become a faithful, constant companion of my real shadow. Just try to think this through and imagine what it means to see only what you want to see. Can you understand that? In a way, this was a kind of training to prepare me for what I would see once I was out of prison. You see, the camera of the human eye needs to be trained. And then retrained, and then retrained again, in accordance with the latest Party line. Do you follow me, Mr Klementini? It wasn't until I ended up in Valdice that I learned to generate a suitable backdrop. And believe me, life without a backdrop is as impossible in Valdice as it is under socialism, or in post-Communist society for that matter. Does it surprise you – you're quite entitled to be surprised – that after an eighteen-hour shift I forced myself to avoid the sight of those black shoes, those brothel creepers? There are things – things that can sometimes last for months – that you can't survive, that you would never survive, you just wouldn't be able to take, unless you built a castle on a chicken leg inside your own head. It doesn't matter what kind of castle, any old castle will do, as long as it's on a chicken leg! The chicken leg is the foundation rock! After all – I'm sure you know this as well as I do – when you're twenty-three you can't survive without a castle on a chicken leg. There, in the catacombs, it would sometimes happen in the mornings – at least to me it did – that together with something resembling coffee in a mess tin, I would be handed a piece of a newspaper. A tiny scrap. Sometimes torn from *Rudé Právo*, sometimes from some other newspaper. For wiping my bottom. And one day the paper – which must have been ripped out of *Květy* or some other women's magazine – had a bit of a picture, and in the light illuminating the cell for the moment when the warder handed me the coffee, I spotted a woman's thigh, a belly and a breast. It might have been the reproduction of a famous painting. Once darkness returned, I couldn't rid myself of the image of that beautiful female thigh, belly and breast. I got an erection and began to masturbate, like a starving man guzzling down his food. I rubbed the scrap of paper – I remember this down to the tiniest detail – with my left hand against my side until the fragment of the image fell apart on my skin. Rats scuttled around, as usual. I couldn't get rid of the compulsive thought that the rats were lapping up my sperm. My proteins. What did you say? Oh yes, I certainly had enough vital juices in me still.

I swear to you, Mr Klementini, that the only way one can survive prison – a place like Valdice Section III, with the catacombs and everything that goes with it, the cherry on the cake – the only way a healthy basketball player could survive was by transforming his head into an adjustable object made of oak, that could be enlarged or shrunk at will by turning a screw, like one of those two-part hat moulds, making it possible for the head to replace the truth with any preposterous, made-up nonsense. The Voice of America also understood what was going on in other kinds of milliners' heads, that's why they used to sign off by wishing their listeners "Good night and good luck!". Do you have any idea how many people the Voice of America helped to build socialism? Every morning the station inspired people to make a dash for the bathroom before rushing to their trolleybus stop and getting on with their day. "Good luck." What inspiring perniciousness!

There was something else that kept me going in Valdice when I was thrown into solitary. Even as a child I loved sitting in the dark. For hours on end. No idea why. It just made me feel happy. I forget what thoughts went through my mind in those days – I mean when I was a little boy. My late father tried in vain to cure me of this bad habit. But this was precisely what stopped me from losing my mind when I first ended up in the hole, in the catacombs, in those damned casemates. You have to tame your environment, even if it consists of nothing but darkness. And rats. And water, ice cold water. But most important, you have to tame time. Time is hard to tame, but it can be done. It depends on the strength of the tamer within you.

Do you understand? I made myself believe that those actual brothel creepers, those feet in stretch socks, the shoes as well as the trousers, were just a figment of my imagination, that I hadn't really seen them, even as I was looking at them. And it was at that very moment that I heard someone coming up to the attic. Someone's hurried steps. It was Vrtiak. Carrying a basket of wet laundry. That's how we met. He nearly crashed into me. And it was only then that I noticed that a white, cast-iron chair lay toppled over quite close to the black shoes dangling in the air. A garden chair belonging to my landlord.

The man hanging there was the landlady's father-in-law. There was something striking about the letter – I haven't mentioned that yet – the letter that the father-in-law had pinned to the beam nearest to the window. Like a flashy visiting card. An invitation. Calligraphic writing on thick paper. After the funeral the landlady read it out to all the tenants. She also told us that lately her father-in-law had been doing the rounds of specialist doctors. Literally besieging them. Complaining about all sorts of aches and pains: in his belly, his chest, near his heart, in his head. Yet – no matter what clever tricks they tried in order to prise the information out of him – he was unable to describe his symptoms, to provide any relevant details of his afflictions. The doctors attended to him, obliged him by referring him for all kinds of tests – because a cousin of his son's was working at the Department of Passports and Visas – but none of the specialists was able to come up with any clear diagnosis.

At the end of his letter, the hanged man claimed – now comes the explanation – that he had absolutely no doubt that he would have received treatment and perhaps even been cured if he had offered a hefty bribe, but that he was not prepared, under any circumstances and at any cost, to do any such thing, since he had never in his life greased anyone's palm. That was why he would rather hang himself than give a doctor even as little as five crowns. Incidentally, the old man, the one who had hanged himself, used to be a businessman. He had made his fortune in the 1930s. By selling flypaper. The landlord and his wife had kept a sample, which they showed us. Then the old man moved on to selling cheap, third-rate agricultural machinery. He would cheat the farmers left, right and centre. Eventually he turned to dealing in sewing machines. And it was he who had built the house; it remains a mystery how and through what connections the old man's son and his wife-to-be ended up working for the secret police. I'm still surprised that they were willing to take me as a lodger when I responded to their ad, and that they didn't kick me out the moment I showed up on their doorstep.

Thank you. That's the kind of compliment I'm always happy to accept. Smoke-curing depends primarily on the wood, obviously, but also on patience, since you're working with smoke. I usually smoke-cure six or seven pike for the winter; it depends. Really? Go on, help yourself: I'm so glad to hear that. Most people make milk-caps with a sour marinade – I like mine this way, slightly charred, then drenched in a salty brine with whole peppercorns.

So, you see, Vrtiak and I met courtesy of a hanged man. That was the beginning of our friendship. He was in the final semester of his pharmaceutical studies and I had come out of prison barely a month earlier. After fifteen years. I found some ghastly job. But it paid well. I was explosives manager – although I wasn't the explosives manager officially. The official explosives manager was somebody quite different. I'm not saying that they didn't train me in how to handle explosives, that certainly wasn't the case. I took the job for the money, as by then I'd been left all alone in this world, except for my sister. I forgot to mention that my father died in prison. That very same Valdice. The two of us were desperate for money. I got the job through a former inmate, a man from Bratislava who had been released six months earlier. Obviously, I bore all the risks that went with the job of an explosives manager. If something had happened, the explosives manager – that is, the official one – and all the other employees would have stuck together. He would have got off scot free, and so would everyone else, leaving me to carry the can, of course. The explosives manager would have blamed me and everyone would have backed him up. Because the blasting was done using the Soviet method. Without a countdown. There was just the one blast. Then you had to go and check if an unexploded charge had been left somewhere. I trust I needn't go into greater detail.

Vrtiak never said anything; he never gave me a crumb of information about his own background, except the thing about his mother's pregnancy and his perfect pitch. Nor did I ever ask any questions.

I was making good money in the quarry although at least twice a week I had to fear for my life. But I had no other option. In those days everyone steered clear of someone like me. And besides: I was in real countryside; it wasn't just a postcard, it was real nature. You can't begin to imagine what it means to be in the countryside for someone who has just spent fifteen years behind bars.

Try to picture this: my eyes would wander around the landscape, my head would turn and every now and then – you won't believe this – it felt as if I were looking at wallpaper, as if I were looking not at a bit of living landscape but a fake, a coloured photograph revolving gradually around my head like a slowly unfurling bolt of fabric; it felt as if something were missing from the landscape – only I didn't know what. The thing that was missing was missing from my own head. That's what was missing! Do you know what I mean? Any number of times I would stand there gazing out into the valley feeling as if what I saw before me was not reality but a plastic replica, as if the landscape couldn't possibly be so beautiful, as if this beautiful landscape couldn't be real. That it was impossible. And that was how I started to get used to an impossibility of another kind.

Vrtiak kept inviting me to go out dancing, partly, I assume, at the instigation of his lady friends, though he didn't get married in the end, but I always turned him down. Until a woman changed everything. How her beauty made me suffer! Her beauty brought me nothing but pain. Darling, what's wrong with you, my dear Adonis?, she asked me as our first night as lovers was about to begin. But when I explained what was actually wrong with her Adonis, she threw herself at me, emitting a curious, loud noise, and began to kiss my withered, wrinkled scrotum sans balls, asking the same question over and over again: how did they do that to you? Her weeping was as prolonged and ostentatious as at a state funeral. She began to lose weight and after a couple of weeks she told me in a café that I should have warned her the first time we met about the mishap I'd had in prison – she claimed that on that night my waltzing had been at least as graceful as

Leonidas's in Werfel's *Pale Blue Ink in a Lady's Hand* – at least that's what she said – but that my behaviour had, in fact, been criminal because I had knowingly, as a responsible adult, allowed her to fall in love with me and become completely besotted. She said I had given her a shock for life.

In some mysterious way Vrtiak found out, although I have never fathomed how, that in 1950 I had been sentenced to eighteen years for high treason, charged with devising a devious, cunning plot to subvert the republic, and that I had been released under Novotný. After my so-called accident. I found his curiosity more hurtful than repellent, as I had no doubt that the only thing he could possibly be really interested in was how I ended up being castrated in Valdice.

One night the two of us went out for a drink – I forget what the occasion was, all I remember is that we got completely hammered in some pub, a seedy dive. It was a little foggy outside. As I sat there, staring out of the window, he asked: Ondrej, is it true that towards the end of your time in Valdice, you dabbled in painting? That a warder wanted you to do his portrait, but he wanted to test you first to see if you could do a likeness, that's how the warder had put it. But instead of giving you a mirror to help you draw yourself, he gave you this ancient, fifty-year-old Riz-Abadie tin that had once contained some tobacco product. The warder held the gleaming bottom of the box in front of you and told you to draw yourself. And you were supposed to capture your own likeness! The warder insisted on that before letting you draw him. I must admit I was shocked to hear Vrtiak say that. I very nearly went for his throat. But I held back. Or rather... something in me held me back. All I did was ask where he came to be so well informed. Cool as a cucumber, he said: Oh, you know, here in Slovakia everyone knows everything. I must have been more drunk than I thought, because I did lose it eventually and started to shout, I asked what it was he wanted to know, yelling that if he had heard the story about the painting, about the Riz-Abadie tin, he was bound to know about my empty scrotum. Was he planning to shout it from the rooftops, I asked. I screamed at him with all the other guests watching, I accused him of not being interested in anything except my balls. No, my balls are no more! I yelled, all there is to see is my little drowned rat! He tried to calm me down: terrible things had happened, everyone would understand that sooner or later.

All of a sudden, I noticed a woman sitting at our table. She was about Vrtiak's age. I have never understood how she ended up at our table and why I hadn't noticed her before. I must have been dead drunk. Soon after, the waiters kicked all three of us out of the pub. The bill was quite steep. And the woman was grey and sad, but beautiful. It was eleven thirty.

It dawned on me that what the pharmacist-to-be and this woman, a complete stranger whom we'd met by chance in that run-down dive, were after was to see with their very own eyes, for a few seconds at least, some compelling evidence, visible evidence, a *corpus delicti*, that would confirm what they had heard. The thing about my balls. We left the pub and headed for a park. Street lighting. I recall the twigs on the trees looking as if they had been twisted out of silver wire. I remember that particular detail precisely, even though I was totally plastered, and I remember what she said: bamboos in bloom. Lately I've been dreaming of blooming bamboos. The kind you can find in an atlas of woody plants. You know, that big German botanical atlas. She turned to Vrtiak and said: Did you know that bamboo blossoms only once in its lifetime, just before it is about to die?

Somebody, one of the two men who left the pub after us – although there is no denying that they were hard-boiled secret policemen – commented as they followed us: anglers who smoke should make sure they wash the nicotine off their hands before attaching the bait to the rod. How can anyone forget such a basic thing! Are there no decent anglers left anymore? We were approaching a streetlamp. So, to put an end to the film show, so to speak, I undid my flies as the fellows in leather jackets slowly passed by. I fished out my unfuelled hero, who was quite reluctant to emerge into the cold, followed by what used to be the pouch for my testes, the furrowed, creased bit of mangled skin. Eva's face – Eva was how Vrtiak addressed her – stiffened. What did you do, the first fellow asked in a coarse, harsh voice. You did this, I replied and thrust my crotch at him. Just then Eva lashed out and slapped the cheek of the man nearest to her. The other one produced the kind of ID I knew only too well, knocking Eva to the ground, and started kicking her. Suddenly he checked himself, gave his colleague a nudge, whispered something in his ear and the two of them began to run towards the park. That was when it first struck me that our friend Hubert might be an informer. Although, in fact, that had already occurred to me when he mentioned the painting.

I remember Eva accidentally biting her lower lip and blood pouring down onto her white mohair scarf. Words fail me when I try to express the look on her face. But I had seen a face like that before. It was a little bit like the face of the dying Russian who had collapsed after drinking all the spirit from a small cylindrical jar that had once contained some kind of preserved snake. During the war, the entire natural science museum, our local museum that is, had been moved to the cellar where we too lay low as we waited for the shooting to end. Some other preservatives must have been added to the spirit.

So now you've seen what you wanted to see, I said as I lifted Eva from the pavement. Vrtiak embraced me – and I was gripped by such fear that I thought I would faint. Vrtiak asked Eva if she was in pain but she shook her head. I seem to remember that her teeth were clenched tight. But she couldn't stand. I went to call an ambulance. She died in hospital. The man had kicked her in the spleen, crushing one of her kidneys. The bamboo blossoms were right. I didn't attend her funeral. And for the next few years I kept well away from Vrtiak as well.

Then I moved to central Slovakia. One day I was trying to get hold of some medication for my sister. I looked for it in every pharmacy, large and small. And that was how I chanced upon Vrtiak again. He managed to procure what I needed, of course. And since then, he and I have shared something – a kind of polite friendship. Very nearly a sincere friendship. We regularly send each other cards. On all sorts of occasions. Name days. Birthdays. Christmas. Letters, too. He is a wonderful man. Except that his curiosity always gets the better of his sincerity. Even today I can't tell whether or not he had been an informer. Does that contradict what I said about him earlier? Maybe not. Well, there we are. So much for Vrtiak.

I know that my stories about Vrtiak may be of absolutely no interest to you. You aren't really interested, are you? Am I right? Well, then. But we will still need him in the future. Keep him in the back of your mind.

My sister and I come from an extremely poor family. I don't know if Vrtiak told you that. My father was a lowly labourer who for many years worked for the railways. Needless to say, he was a long-standing member of the Communist Party. After February 1948 he rose to be chairman of the local party cell. Early in 1959, around Carnival time, my father suddenly became disgruntled. At home, too, he began to grumble about everything. In fact, he had been disgruntled for some time, but up till then he had kept it to himself.

Someone, perhaps it was the station master, came up with the idea of a ball. A ball during the Carnival season – nothing unusual about that, but it was the sort of thing my father had never cared for. But he was persuaded to attend the ball in his capacity as Party chairman. I heard they put him under as much pressure as if he'd been a dyed-in-the-wool *kulak* refusing to join the co-operative, as we used to say. There was a note at the bottom of the poster inviting people to the ball: *Formal dress compulsory*. Compulsory – this only two years after the Communist victory. People still reeked of capitalism, to coin a phrase. And so our entire family – me, the printer's apprentice, my sister, my mother and my aunt took my father's measurements, double-checked them and set out to find something resembling a dinner jacket. A double-breasted one, like the one Comrade Klement Gottwald used to wear. Complete with white shirt and bow tie.

We began to get my father ready for the ball in our new flat in the brand new block where the smoke didn't make its way into the chimneys properly and the whitewash on the walls left marks on everything we touched. We got the size right and my father looked splendid in the off-the-peg double-breasted suit. Except for his hands which, next to the bow tie, looked like huge protuberances on a tree.

As my father walked into the hall where the ball was about to begin, he was welcomed by applause. Long Live the Communist Party of Czechoslovakia, and other slogans in this vein. Then came the chanting: Long Live Comrade Ostarok! Stalin, Gottwald, Široký, may they live forever! More chanting followed, for several minutes: Long Live Comrade Ostarok! Father delivered his opening speech. He said that in the old days only rich people could go to balls, and so on and so forth. He had learned his speech by heart. It was written by my sister, then still at high school, who had cobbled it together from paragraphs found in various pamphlets. So far so good. The trouble was that people knew my father's old weakness and someone brought a bottle of homemade slivovitz. My father had quite a lot to drink and people gathered round him. And my father's tongue loosened. I kept an eye on him as best I could, but I wasn't able to stop him. Before midnight he limited himself to the odd mumbling comment about this or that member of the regional party committee, but as time went on, he started badmouthing everyone he could think of. Loudly, no holds barred. As he downed one shot after another, the crowd around him kept growing, watching him gesticulate wildly, as if trying to emulate a neighbour of ours, an amateur actor usually cast in dramatic roles in plays by Ferko Urbánek. He declared, almost at the top of his voice, that very difficult times lay ahead for the working classes, whose rights he had been defending all his life. Leaning forward as if preparing to dive into a swimming pool, arms outstretched, hands clasped together, he pointed to the door and announced that the working class was destined for a black door. The silence that fell was so thick you could have cut it with a knife, like a bowl of aspic. Suddenly all his clothes felt too tight, he shouted that people couldn't even make shirts properly anymore, and he kept wanting to loosen his shirt collar, complaining that it was trying to throttle his speech, and by the time he yanked off his bow tie he was surrounded by a throng of people; even some of the band joined in, I remember a saxophonist sitting cross-legged by my father's feet, his saxophone slung across his shoulder like a gun. Some of his most loyal friends tried to stop him from downing yet another shot of slivovitz and hid the bottle, but three more bottles appeared from somewhere. My father climbed onto a chair, inadvertently ruffling his hair and fingering his ears with trembling hands, and declared that banning books was wrong, that people should be allowed to read whatever they wanted, including stuff written by deviationists, that everyone with a proper class instinct would immediately understand what made Bukharin, Kamenev, Zinoviev and Trotsky deviationists – all you needed was a good Communist's nose. He also insisted that, if he could, he would have the key works of Bukharin and Trotsky printed right now, around the corner or in the carriage of a train, to give people a chance of seeing with their own eyes the errors of their ways. He said he knew where to find people who would help him get these writings printed – I wish my father hadn't said that since, after all, it was common knowledge that I was a printer's apprentice. He went on to say that only people with a class instinct were able to grasp the truth of any particular historical period. He stressed that Christ had been a carpenter, meaning he had come from a working-class family, had working-class origins, and that if back then, two thousand years ago, he had had the support of the proletariat and the slaves, everything would have turned out differently. The rich would have disappeared! At that point someone shouted: a right mess you've got yourself into! A few young boys in the gallery started to imitate the hooting of an owl. No one could drag my father away. He seemed to be possessed. My mother sprained her ankle running away from him. I knew we were in trouble. I drank myself into a stupor on some terribly sweet liqueur and I don't remember how the evening ended. My father was arrested the following day and a few days later they came for me as well. The main charge against me was that I was planning to help publish anti-Soviet writing.

Don't worry, I'm not going to bang my head against a brick wall again. I suspect there are no more shocking facts left to be revealed about Valdice and Section III. There is just one thing perhaps that no one has ever talked about: whether anyone had been held in solitary, in the catacombs, for as long as three hundred days. And if so, whether that person had survived. Three hundred days may not sound like a lot to you, but it does to me.

On my name day, St Andrew's day, a new warder arrived. Fenykel was his name. I couldn't help observing him during roll call. I don't know how he felt about me staring at him but I do know how I was affected by his eyes that glinted like the tremulous flight of a moth: I just knew that if he could, he would have killed me on the spot, there and then, on the first day. He kept yelling at me and accused me of mocking him with my eyes. I asked the prison commander if it was possible to mock someone with one's eyes, but the commander said that

Fenykel simply knew that I intended to offend him. And that one could indeed offend just by looking.

Towards the end of my sentence, despite having a clean record inside, the warder succeeded in having me charged with sedition and I was sentenced to a hundred days' solitary, in the catacombs. According to the regulations, prisoners could not be held there for longer than sixty days. After sixty days they had to move you back into the company, as they used to say in the army, to get your breath back, as they put it, before sending you down to serve your next forty days. Or sixty. Or however many.

In solitary you are absolutely forbidden to lie down. Reveille is, I mean was, before four in the morning. The stench. The water trickling down the walls. The rats crawling out of the pit latrine, and if you were so exhausted that you fell asleep during the day, they'd beat you viciously until they drew blood. But none of that is exactly news: people have been known to experience this: some in one way, others in another. But worse was to come: I didn't know that the fellow who had me sent down to solitary was a homo. And the worst thing was that once a week, or sometimes twice, another homo would impose himself on me. He was a warder or, in fact, a secret policeman. A well-fed bull he was. Strong. He was up to all sorts of tricks. He would lunge at my backside with his cock erect. I don't know how, I have no explanation for it to this day, perhaps the body has its own autonomous intelligence, completely independent of what our brain is thinking; in any case, the bull failed to get into my anus even though he kept attacking it with his cock the way you might try to ram a double gate. He was literally howling while he was at it – and in those moments I imagined the surprised bodies and faces of the girls I had loved in the past. But one day I couldn't take it anymore. I still don't know what it was that I did. In a nutshell: yet again, he had failed to open my anus with that cudgel of his. But I must have done something bad, failed to control myself, because I woke up in a psychiatric hospital. In Prague. In ward seventeen. For prisoners. The psychiatrist didn't believe me that a warder, or rather a warder's cock, could have tried to penetrate me, like some relentless battering ram, and not just once but many times, so they dismissed it as a fantasy. I had lost both balls and was unable to explain how it happened. Nor did they say a word about it either.

Mr Klementini, I would really like to give you an account of what happened to me when my father's rehabilitation finally got under way, to tell you about the terrible poverty my sister was plunged into, but what would be the point? I'm sure you know all that. We received some financial compensation on behalf of our father. I also got some for myself. I decided – or rather, my sister convinced me – to study law, in spite of everything. By then I was no longer working for the state quarry and had found a job at the waterworks.

And one day something I could never have hoped for arrived: my graduation. My sister and I went to Café Krym and as we sat there alone with a couple of bouquets on a third chair, an elderly gentleman suddenly joined us, without asking for permission. He even brought over a chair from another table. I asked him why he didn't ask if he could join us. I was upset but he just smirked as if he was going to tell a joke. Then he addressed Marienka, my sister, by name. Seeing my surprise, he congratulated me on my graduation and ordered a round of drinks. Soon I discovered that he had come purely out of respect, reverence even, for my father. And that's when I learned that he was the chairman of the Regional Communist Party committee.

He asked if I had any particular job in mind now that I had a law degree, and I said I did not. Then he fixed me with his eyes like someone checking out a second-hand car, lowered his voice and continued to ask questions: I understand that you had your cock smashed. At that point Marienka burst into tears. She cried so hard that not just her whole body but also the table she was holding onto began to shake. I asked how he knew that this was my graduation day. He replied, as Vrtiak once did, that in this country you could find out anything provided you knew who to ask. Then he blushed and said something along the lines of: it doesn't matter in the least that you did time because of your father; the Party knows how to make amends. It doesn't matter at all that you've been behind bars, the only thing that matters is – at this point he leaned towards me grabbing, indeed squeezing my wrist – what matters is that working-class blood runs in your veins! Working-class blood – I will never forget those words till the day I die. Neither the Party nor your blood will ever forget what you've been through. You are ready – even if you're not a Party member. Everything in good time.

That same day he walked Marienka and me to a hotel and took out a portable Consul and proceeded to type up, with his own two fat index fingers, my application for a job in the Ministry of Interior's archives, which, of course, he worded himself. I could barely keep myself from bursting out laughing when I heard him dictate the application to himself. But I did get the job. Contrary to all logic. And a decent salary to boot. And I'm still here today. My sister would come and visit me here every now and then – she didn't live far, some ninety kilometres away. She used to bring me all kinds of preserves. It wasn't until later that I discovered, through various channels, that this man, this benefactor of mine, had been one of the people who was forced to testify against my father – but I also learned that he was the only one whose reputation remained unsullied through the dozens of show trials and that later, in the aftermath of the Twentieth Congress of the Communist Party of the Soviet Union, this was what propelled him to rise to become the most powerful man in the Party in central Slovakia and its unchallenged eminence grise.

Regent is staring at me again. The best way to describe his gaze is calm and profoundly compassionate, almost dignified. But I noticed that the fur on his back was bristling again very slightly.

We'll get there in the end, Mr Klementini, don't worry, I'm not wasting your time. Your case and that of your family is no gossip column tittle-tattle, it was sheer villainy, even though your father's trial wasn't major enough to make headlines at the time. I've seen the file. I know that you are looking for something in particular – but if you want to learn something more about your case, you also need to know something else. If you think this is a waste of your time and that everything can be planned the way one plans the building of a house, the bringing of a child into this world, a holiday in Mexico, and so forth, you are wrong. That is why I suggest that you either partake of this kirsch, or that we part ways.

Agreed? Right, let's have another shot. To your good health. Thank you. OK, to mine as well.

Where was I? Ah, yes, so Vrtiak came to see me here, then he came again and then yet again, for a third time. At first, he went about it in a roundabout way. But eventually he came clean: Ondrej, do you, by any chance, know something about the case of a raid on an aircraft factory? Some people – quite a perfectionist lot they were – received an order to organize the raid. I believe they were policemen in disguise. It happened in the middle of 1948: they barged in during a night shift, drew their guns and held up the staff while several of them pounced on the paperwork. They took everything, along with some spare parts for aircraft engines. To cut a long story short, the entire documentation vanished. And the perpetrators also vanished into thin air, like in a fairy tale, along with their lorry. Phones were out of order all night. Apart from a routine investigation, nothing much happened during the eighteen months or so after the raid. Your father was not arrested until after Slánský. That's what Vrtiak told me, and I recalled the case immediately. I've seen the file. Vrtiak then told me that the father of a friend of his, called Klementini, took the blame. He was sentenced to death because he had been the manager in charge of the factory after nationalisation. Soon after, his wife was executed as well. And so Vrtiak asks me: can you help his son, the son of this engineer, Klementini? Vrtiak went on to say that his friend – that is, you – was one hundred per cent certain that someone had planned the raid in advance. A complete stranger appeared in court to testify against your father and claimed that he, that is your father, had received 90,000 US dollars for looking the other way. Apparently, the dollars had been discovered by Nosek's people in a spare tyre in your father's garage. But apparently he – that is you – knew that your father hadn't taken any money, and also that the raid had been a sham. In court your father stated in his defence that he didn't own a spare tyre, but to no avail. All the witnesses – a cleaner, a neighbour, and eventually, after a bit of a beating, even your mother – testified that they had seen a spare tyre in the garage. The main charge against him was that he had been in contact with US intelligence and helped the newly established Jewish state to arm itself, although your father wasn't even Jewish. Nor was your mother. 90,000 US dollars were displayed on the desk on the day the hearing opened to the public. Even the tyre was there as an additional exhibit. Allegedly, the raid had been carried out by capitalist mercenaries of the Jewish state who had been born here in Czechoslovakia, and your father, Mr Klementini, was alleged to have facilitated the shipping of the stolen goods.

So, as you see, I am familiar with the case. However, we can't discuss it unless you learn more about some other court cases, so that you can compare your father's trial with other, much more baffling ones, and see it, so to speak, in the context of the state madness that reigned at the time.

I am not at all surprised, Mr Klementini, that you were unable to find any trace of your father's file anywhere. In Prague or in Bratislava. So this was by way of an introduction, before we go into more detail.

I had been working here for some time – well, long enough – when I met a colonel in state security. I vowed never to reveal the colonel's identity to anyone. Names are immaterial anyway. He is no longer with us. Forgotten. The only thing I knew was that he was a big shot. And I also heard that as a young officer, soon after Clementis was hanged, he had been swiftly dispatched from Prague to Bratislava and was later transferred from Bratislava to this place. He must have known something about me, but even if he didn't, he is sure to have known about my father. That he had died in Valdice prison. And also what had happened to my mother and how my sister had been treated before my father was rehabilitated. He must also have seen my job application for the position here in the archive. The colonel's signature would decide: a yes or a no. The colonel used to arrive by car, his driver would pull into the courtyard and armed policemen would stand guard as the files were unloaded and carried upstairs. The colonel accompanied every batch. Once everything had been carried upstairs, the documents would be checked one more time, filed in their proper place in the security safes and "locked up to the teeth" – as people used to say hereabouts, in our neck of the woods. And the colonel would slap the seals on. He would check all the other seals too, the old seals on the safes, then he'd wave goodbye and be gone. That is how it went, year after year. He had started here as a very young lieutenant and rose to the rank of colonel. And a colonel he remained until the day he died.

One day something important happened: the engine in the colonel's car conked out. Just as they were about to leave. Everyone did his best to help. Including my driver, I mean, the castle driver. I was also responsible for the castle museum, you see. But my primary responsibility was for the archives. I answered for it with my life. Day and night. You won't believe it but a single phone call was enough: comrade, you are hereby notified that this or that has happened, and everything, lightbulbs included, would immediately spring to attention. No sooner had something stirred somewhere – a crisis in Afghanistan, for example – over here, in the middle of the forest, far away from Afghanistan, all the lights would come on and I had to do the rounds of the whole archives twice every night, get the gun ready, try every door handle and check every single door that I had personally locked only a couple of hours earlier. Some kind of sabotage was expected all the time. Where were we, anyway? Oh yes, the engine in the colonel's car conked out. The colonel's driver got to carry the can. The dead engine was one matter, but the real problem was a broken part – I don't know about cars and never have, so I can't say what the part was called, even though we kept banging on about it for a long time afterwards. In any case, the chances that my driver could fix it were close to zero. The nearest garage is a good sixteen kilometres away. Eventually I managed to get hold of an Avia truck to tow the colonel's car. The colonel stayed behind. I forget what we talked about but eventually the colonel asked me to give him a tour of the castle, as he rarely had time for outings. Yes, Mr Klementini, I understand, time is of the essence. But even time has to bide its time.

You know what, Ondrej – this is more or less what the colonel said to me as we walked around the castle – there's a cooperative here in the vicinity where they breed trout. How about I drop by some day to pick up a kilo or two and we can have a proper chat. He switched to my first name and said I should do likewise. The colonel moved slowly, examining the stuffed animals carefully, literally in every detail. He paused in front of each animal, giving almost imperceptible nods. Suddenly, when I least expected it, he turned his head abruptly and violently, fixing me with his gaze. It felt as if he had placed invisible weights on my eyes. That was when I realized that his gaze would never yield to the force of someone else's gaze. Only to his own self-destructive urges. It was as if the pupils, irises and whites of his eyes enabled him to observe everything from a different angle. As if he were staring out from a place from which most other people would never be able to look at anything.

Suddenly the colonel declared: what's the point of stuffing animals? It's unspeakably sad. Stuffing animals – taxidermy – isn't there something incredibly hideous about that? Then he leaned close to me and asked in a whisper: what if all these animals were Party members and that's what is preventing them from moving? They can't make a move because they've been stuffed by the Communist Party and the government. I froze and let out a scream. I remember it was a wordless scream, like when you're having teeth pulled. I was overcome by horror. By horror and bewilderment. For I realized that the colonel's provocative question was insiduous in a premeditated and deliberate way.

It took me a very, very long time to start to believe that the colonel really and truly didn't believe in Communism. Some time later the colonel confided in me: I used to be a Communist. Like your father. You can't imagine what things were like when I left for France with my parents and brother. My palate had completely forgotten what normal bread was like. We used to drink water that tasted of rust. We went in search of seasonal work. As seasonal labourers. World War II broke out. We were no longer welcome. My father was in and out of prison. You probably don't not know that my first job was with the criminal police. I loved everything about that line of work. Then I was admitted to the Party as the son of an old Communist. A Communist who used to pick up cigarette butts from the pavement for Viliam Široký. Yes, things like that happened as well. Working for the criminal department taught me to read people's eyes. I managed to solve a few cases. Our pot-bellied grandmas with guns in their belts cheered: what an achievement! So young and already so clever! But afterwards, when the Warsaw Pact barged into this country, I got fed up with this socialism of ours.

I had never heard anyone curse the regime the way he did.

Well, about ten days later the colonel came back, to pick up some trout. We continued our conversation. I served him pike in red wine and he suggested we go and look at some of the most highly classified files. He arrived equipped with everything needed for the safes, just like when he came to open, close and seal them. He reminded me several times that I would not believe him until I'd read some of the stark facts for myself. That was how I also came across your father's indictment, Mr Klementini.

Yes, I am familiar with the facts of your case. But first, let me stimulate your palate with something of greater significance: something related to our history, that is, the history of the former Czechoslovakia, after 1948. Listen to this: there's the Soviet secret service, happily talking to US intelligence, top brass to top brass obviously, about the issue of the life or death of a certain politician. One party, let's say it's the Americans, is not particularly keen that he should die, although it fits in very conveniently with their double encircling manoeuvre aimed at whipping up anti-Soviet sentiment in the West, which would allow them to make several major, even invaluable, moves which in turn would enable them to stall on other matters, in those cases where they think the Soviets would not immediately pounce on an opportunity to make this move or that on the chessboard, or be aware of the potential consequences of the variations on this or that move, and might thus miss their opportunities to make further moves. The other party, the Communists from the U-ES-ES-R, badly need this politician to die, they are in need of this card, since they know – and they know full well! – that their adversary has that card in his hand. It's not a low card, not a dud! On the contrary, it's an ace! But the man cannot be disposed of just like that. The top brass discuss the matter. Now listen carefully and mark my words. The subject of this discussion, however, is not the card that both sides must sacrifice, for opposing reasons. As a result, our card, the minister, this sensitive and cheerful man is reduced to something less than a lackey, he is reduced to the two-dimensional lackey on the card. The gods behind the scenes steer the conversation away from that particular card, but they keep circling back to said card, the said ace, albeit in such a way as if they didn't care about it at all, while at the same time both parties assure each other obliquely, by means of various courteous distractions and hints, of their unwavering respect for the Soviet sphere of influence, the sphere of our garlanded ally, our comrade in arms, that's what I really meant to say. But while the Soviets need absolute certainty, some kind of receipt, a certificate – the Americans actually have that certainty, they know what the

Soviets want to do, they know that the Soviets want to hear 'yes' in reply to a question that has never actually been posed, they understand what makes the diplomats from the melancholy empire of birch forests tick, an empire where the tiger and the lamb share a single soul. Except that the Soviets wouldn't be Soviets if their diplomatic language did not resemble layers in the veneer of 10-mm thick plywood. A renaissance language. Meanwhile, in expectation of some verbal confirmation, of an absence of ambiguity, the atmosphere has become far too fraught. So the Americans get up and take their leave. And guess what happens a few days later? The minister, the chubby minister, tumbles out of a narrow window. They tried to teach him how to fly. The file relating to this case has never been kept here, but I heard all about it from the colonel. And the way this card fell was perfect. The United States won: throughout the Western world resentment of Russia rocketed. And Stalin, meanwhile, Stalin cemented his *soyuz* with Czechoslovakia. Well, how about another drink, huh?

The documents I came across in this archive included a shocking file – had it not been for the colonel I'd never have believed that anything like that was possible: our Vlado Clementis was hanged on 3 December 1952. I presume that the German diplomats in East Berlin, sly foxes that they were, wanted to sniff out the mood among our country's big shots. Find out what effect these executions had on our big beasts of prey. They phoned Bacílek, the Minister for State Control, at his home to ask if they could pay the comrade a brief visit and take the liberty of offering him a small gift, as they happened to be passing through our country, and so on. They were met with a warm, maybe even glowing, assurance that they would be more than welcome, of course. The phones started ringing off the hook. Comrades, what do we need so soon after the first December executions? What better than some visiting Germans? Brilliant! Get hold of a film crew double quick! And scoot up to Bacílek's villa. Up the hill, up the hill, to the miller's weir! Hey ho, to the miller's weir! I have to tickle myself to make myself laugh because it's making me sick to the pit of my stomach.

Top of the agenda: a state and party delegation from the GDR is dropping in on Comrade Bacílek on their way home! Filmmakers, step on it! Put the pedal flat down. It's all done and dusted. And now for the contents of the actual file: a young documentary filmmaker and his cameraman board an official Tatraplán car, you know, otherwise known as the metal dinner jacket or the fish, and race up to Comrade Minister's house. A bodyguard makes a phone call. Our film crew waits. Eventually they are led into a drawing room of sorts and that's as far as they got. Their eyeballs popped out. There on the carpet lay Comrade Minister of State Control Karol Bacílek with his visitors from the German Democratic Republic, surrounded by a vast array of intricate railway tracks with model trains on them. The toy trains hurtled down pasteboard hills, through tunnels, across bridges and along viaducts, past miniature houses and railway stations. Comrade Minister Bacílek was ecstatic about the train set the German comrades brought. The trains ran up and down the tracks while Mrs Bacílek personally served sauerkraut soup in overflowing bowls of white china. She set each bowl on the floor in front of the German guests – her husband already had one in front of him –

while the film crew had to hold their hot bowls in their hands and eat standing up. The documentary film-maker didn't forget to comment – this was the only mitigating circumstance – that the soup was outstanding and the sausage tasted delicious, too. The hostess was assisted by one of the bodyguards who carried a tray with an assortment of vodkas from one guest to the next. Bowing to each member of the delegation in turn, he placed a glass next to the aluminium tracks as a model of the latest East German express sped by. There was no filming and the crew left appalled and the worse for wear. Later that day the film director gave someone a humorous account of the evening and three months later he was sentenced to three years' imprisonment for deliberately disparaging and mocking a state and party official. That's how dangerous realism can be. Those were the days. You could be invited somewhere to see something and end up in jail for seeing it.

So now you can understand that had it not been for the colonel, I'd never have laid eyes on a single file kept in those safes and rather than a custodian of human perfidy I would have remained a lowly guard dog of steel boxes. You would never believe – I'm getting to the file you're interested in, your father's indictment – the kinds of wrappings truth can come in. What if – what if it was your mother who had contributed most to your father's death? The trouble is that in the end something else prevailed over her love for your father. And, as a result, she also ended up on the gallows for it. Best leave it there, don't you think? It's going to rain, I can feel it in my bones. Perhaps you're happy to be on the verge of securing the information you've been seeking for years. But as a matter of fact, you'd be better off not being so happy.

Just then Regent barked twice, ran over to the door, and started to sniff at the crack between the ancient woodwork and the doorframe.

Follow me, I said, and led Klementini down a corridor to a large room lined with security safes. The first thing he noticed was that the plastic seals were missing. I took a set of keys out of my pocket and started opening one safe after another. Every single one of them was empty. I felt the weight of Klementini's gaze. His eyes, darting about the spiky void inside the dark olive-coloured safes, seemed to flutter like a bird locked in a cage for the first time. As we walked from safe to safe, I asked:

How good are you at reading air? – It's been stored here as in a kilner jar. It has lost none of its smell or savour and never will, even if I left the safes wide open all day long. Environmentalists in the West have tried to analyse air that was three hundred years old. They have unscrewed some old binoculars, ancient compasses, I'm sorry but it makes me laugh. Just try and inhale some of the air of this safe! The old air just stays in there, you can't get it out. It has eaten into the khaki paint. It has corroded the metal carapace. The steel. No, I didn't mean to pull the wool over your eyes! I've told you everything I remember from your parents' file. And now, let's have some kirsch before the final leg of our journey.

Klementini yelled out and grabbed my arms just above my wrists with both hands, but I just gave a faint smile and calmly continued, even though Regent kept growling menacingly: I've got the keys to the garage here, we'll take the Land Rover, the castle's Land Rover – you do drive, don't you? – and we'll go over to where these files have ended up.

I needed a short break. I sat down to catch my breath and then continued, as I gently ran my fingers through the fur between Regent's ears: so, now you're about to learn the crucial piece of information, without which nothing I've said so far would make any sense. Then you will understand that for you it's actually been a blessing in disguise that you haven't got your hands on the file sooner, before this day, this hour and this minute. It will certainly be better for you to let me tell you and show you where the file is now. The only thing we'll encounter is death. In person. It's best that you don't know what your mother said under questioning, from the first interrogation to the last.

So, it is 1989. The Velvet Revolution. It was all change, before the year was out. I was here on my own. I never went out, not even to the shops. The entire staff of the Museum of National History had taken a holiday. My driver didn't show up either, although he wasn't on holiday. There was no cleaner either. My only source of information about what was going on in the country was Radio Free Europe. None of my former visitors dropped by. The phone never rang. Because in the past people working at various state institutions used to come over. The Institute of State and Law, for example – their archives are further down that corridor. Nothing there would be of any use to you, though. It all happened out of the blue two or three days before New Year. It was a rainy day. I think Havel was already president by then. One night, I'm woken up by some ghastly ringing of the doorbell. I get up, slip on my corduroys, grab my gun and cock it – you never know if you'll get the chance to shoot first – and head for the gate, without putting my shoes on, just in my slippers. You're quite unsteady in slippers. What if I hear a voice I recognize, open the gate and someone jumps on my bare feet in clodhoppers or boots? I raise my right hand, the one with the gun. It has happened before – an inspection sprung on me in the middle of the night – I've been dragged out of bed in the early hours many times, but never before have I forgotten my shoes. I must confess: something didn't feel right.

Who's there? I asked when I reached the inner bailey. I was still twenty metres away from the outer one. Open up! Ministry of the Interior! It was a stranger's voice at the entryphone. Who are you?, I asked. After a moment's silence, I heard a familiar voice. The colonel's. So I went and opened the gate. The colonel was standing outside with five other men. Every one of them, including the colonel, looked as if they hadn't slept a wink, or had been on a bender. All wide-eyed. Grubby. Unwashed. And behind them stood two standard-issue military lorries covered in tarpaulin. I noticed they had shields mounted on the headlights – the light was coming out of narrow rectangular slits, as when a battalion is on alert. The colonel gives me a wink and says: We need to get something done double quick. So I say, go ahead. It starts to rain harder, and I say: We'll freeze to death out here. Either you come in or you leave. You're not going to throw us out, are you?, asks the colonel, with a laugh. Then, clearing his throat, he goes on: We have to move some of the archive. So I say: Be my guest. But first let me see the paperwork. The colonel leans close to me, so close that our noses are touching, and says: Have you completely lost your marbles? Paperwork? Haven't you been listening to Radio Free Europe? What planet are you on? Havel is president and they're going to string us up. Who do you think will sign off on it? I can do that, no problem! You have nothing to worry about. We'll just shove a few crates onto the lorries, just the most important stuff, and you won't need to worry about anything else. And you're coming with us, but first you'll lock up here. We'll bring you back tomorrow. All right, I say, but what if someone else comes tomorrow – someone like you lot, and gives me a bollocking? To which he, the colonel, says: I suppose that could happen! Prick up your ears, pin them right back: If they do come, here is what you'll say. You'll tell them that some men from the Ministry of the Interior in Bratislava turned up last night – as indeed we just have – but remember to say that two of them were definitely Czech, although they made an effort to speak Slovak but had a strong Czech accent, that they showed you some official-looking *bumazhkas*, stamped and signed, et cetera, et cetera, and all you did was let them take delivery, and that you're a man of honour.

The colonel was unsteady on his feet but the way he spoke didn't betray quite how drunk he was. I noticed that every one of them, including the colonel, wore a VPN badge. They were all in plain clothes, of course. And the colonel continued the briefing: You must say that the men from Bratislava behaved decently in every other respect, d'you hear! Say that they ordered you to take them to the safes, then they broke the seals, and that some other men who came with them – remember what you've got to say? – these other men then piled all the files onto the lorries. And then off they went – as quickly as they came – and you'll be the one who sets off the alarm first thing tomorrow morning because you will ring the Ministry of the Interior and tell them what happened. They will send three or four officers, maybe more – by now I realised that all of the men standing before me were quite drunk – they'll draw up a report and that'll be that. You'll show them this piece of paper – he stuck a forged Ministry of Interior authorization into my hand – and end of story! You can bet your sweet life they're not going to come after you with the hounds.

You should have seen them working their arses off. They worked at a dizzying speed. And it wasn't just the safes they emptied but also some of the ordinary filing cabinets with regular locks. The colonel had a piece of paper with a list of files to take. There must have been more than five crateloads. They carried everything down to the lorries at a fast trot. Once it was all loaded up, I wanted to go back and put my shoes on, I'd completely forgotten that I was wearing only my slippers. But the colonel yelled: Move it, get on the lorry! There'll be plenty of time to put your shoes on before you die! Toss your gun over the gate, lock up and come along, double quick!

So I swung a leg over the side and got under the tarpaulin. Light was provided by three carbide lamps. A pile of Spiš *borovička* bottles lay on a folded blanket. And something was splashing about inside two yellow, plastic ten-litre gas canisters. A rubber hose was wrapped around one of them. Another hose, submerged in a third canister, was passed around from mouth to mouth. Each of the men – there were about a dozen of them sitting there – took a swig from the canister and squeezed the end of the hose tight before passing it to the next man. Finally it was my turn. It was home-made slivovitz. At least as strong as the kirsch we're drinking now. After a while I had a powerful sense that all these men, that the faces of all these men on the lorry reminded me of some people. They resembled men I knew only too well from somewhere. I could have sworn blind that I'd come across these people somewhere before. Meanwhile the hose came round again and that's when I realized that in this light there was something about these men that made them resemble, in some fundamental, crucial way, the warders in Valdice at the time of Stalin's death. I couldn't believe what I was seeing. I thought it must be some kind of black magic, that I was hallucinating, that I was befuddled and seeing things. I placed my hand on my holster, craned my neck and stared into their faces, into each of these men's faces one by one, fixing each of them for at least five seconds, and I was gripped by a sense of horror, as if on the verge of paralysis. Just like the day Stalin died: the same despair, the same dreadful fear, the same crass grief was imprinted on every single one of these faces, like an indelible official stamp.

No, you mustn't think that I waited for them to ask why I was staring at them like that – that never crossed my mind. But for some reason, that will remain a mystery until the day I die, I have no idea what it was that made me say out loud: I say – haven't we met somewhere before? Quite a few of the men, perhaps all of them, nodded in agreement. Great slivovitz, I said, and they nodded again. We'd been driving for over an hour and yet I didn't have the faintest idea where we were headed or where we were at this moment, even though I'm quite familiar with the roads and the mountains in this neck of the woods. Foraging for mushrooms – that's my thing. The road went up and then, suddenly, down again, a sharp bend followed by what felt like a U-turn. By the time we came to a halt it was well after midnight. We clambered down from the lorry. Our bodies refused to obey our heads. I looked around: it was somewhere I'd never been before. Carbide lamps. And facing the lamps, and also facing me, a huge pit, about six metres by four. The men standing around it, presumably the ones who had dug it – many were still holding shovels and spades – were quite old. I was taken aback. Judging by their faces they had nothing to do with the Ministry of the Interior and must have been at it since early morning. I found it hard to believe that these old men could have dug a pit this big.

The twelve who had been sitting under the tarpaulin with me, along with some of the men who'd come on the first lorry, the colonel's crew, started unloading the files as well as some barrels – barrels filled with quicklime, as it turned out – and at that point the colonel put his hand gently on my shoulder and steered me towards the pit. So I'm standing there with my eyes popping out, I remember feeling the urge to scream but I covered my mouth, grabbing hold of that scream of mine: the pit was filled to the brim with human skeletons. Skeleton upon skeleton. Poking out of the clay, washed clean by the rain that had been pouring steadily, ceaselessly, all day. And here and there beneath the skeletons I caught a glimpse of something else. In the light of the carbide lamps the bones had the colour of dried and faded bay leaves. You've seen it. Now you've seen it, said the colonel in a soft voice, and you know what it means. No one moved. And the colonel continues: let's have a bite first. After all, what kind of funeral is it without a wake. The smell of wet clay hung desolately in the air. The colonel took me over to a tent I hadn't noticed before. A huge Baba Yaga camping tent, which was all lit up inside. Slices of Nitran salami, huge chunks the size of ripe ears of corn, were laid out on two small crates. Some of the men had already gone in, though not the ones who had arrived on the same lorry as me. They each took a silent swig of slivovitz, grabbed a slice of salami and some ham from army packs, and a slice of white bread. Home-made bread. The old men, the ones who had dug the pit – some of them must have been pushing seventy – helped themselves to food and slivovitz, like everyone else. You could hear everyone chewing. The powerful smell of clay mingled with the musty stench of the tarpaulin. I was amazed at the amount of slivovitz these old men were able to put away. They were all perfectly steady on their feet. Every one of these old men looked as focused as if they were doing a crossword puzzle. Then some of the carbide lamps around the pit started flickering. I noticed there were bullet holes in the foreheads of some of the skulls. But I saw only a few skulls from the front. And then the files started to rain down on the skeletons. Some of them contained your mother's testimony, Mr Klementini. In a matter of minutes the skeletons were covered in a layer of files. Next it was the turn of the quicklime. Once the skeletons were covered by the files, a surge of fresh strength seemed to animate the old men exhausted by the digging. I just stood there gaping and gasping. A layer of documents, then a layer of lime. And again, like layers in a cake. In less than a couple of hours it was all over. Not a trace remained. Rolls of the original turf were re-laid on the clay that had been thrown in and were tamped down. The old men moved as if in a speeded-up film. I'd never have expected them to be quite so nimble.

One day, about a month after the execution of the files, or rather, after the funeral and the wake, anyway, after that

God-awful night – I'm sure you get my drift – I was at the hospital in Banská Bystrica and there I happened to bump into a person who shall remain nameless. The colonel. We both ended up on the same ward for the treatment of our burnt ankles. He asked me – once we were finished at the hospital – whether I still recalled everything, whether I still hadn't learned how to forget. It was a gloomy day, the fog was as thick as boiled starch: everything – the trees, the streets, the two of us, the entire Urpín Hill – was drenched in starch.

All of a sudden, the colonel turns to me and says: I've reached the end of my picture book. What picture book, I ask. Just a picture book, he says. Any old picture book: about a fox, or a badger. A mole, a hedgehog, a giraffe – wouldn't it be wonderful if, once our lives come to an end, we could, with our last breath, step straight into the picture book we most loved when we were young. We'd be two-dimensional, but we'd be happy. Eternal life in a book of animal stories for children – that was what he longed to find in the next world as the ultimate absolution, if indeed there is such a thing. He asked me to check into a local hotel instead of catching a train home and to let him know where I was staying so he could arrange a telephone meeting with me. I didn't ask any questions and did as he said. After returning home from the hospital he shot himself, naked in the bathtub; he chose to do it in the bathroom to save his wife having to clean up after him, as he said in the note that he left. But I would learn that only later. Perhaps he wouldn't have shot himself if his wife and child had been at home. Something else I wasn't aware of was that his wife had a lover who wanted to marry her, son and all. Not a good idea for someone of the colonel's age.

But before he shot himself, we had a long conversation over the phone. He told me, among other things, that I needn't worry about the burial of the files anymore since the old men who had so obligingly dug the pit, the secret mass grave, were the same – at that time young – men who had shot and buried fifty-odd people in the same place in 1944. I had known about the bodies in the pit for years, said the colonel, but I kept my mouth shut. The information was as safe with me as in a Swiss bank. I hoped to put them on trial some day. I knew where they lived. So I invited them to do this one-off job because I had an inkling that there would never be a trial. I thought this would be a kind of a memento for them, but it had precisely the opposite effect. Ever since then they have all been able to get a good night's sleep.

Do you know what will happen now that it's all over? the colonel on the phone went on. I won't be around anymore, but you can bet your sweet life that what I say will come to pass. Every word. Once I'm buried, a fresh investigation will be opened. An investigation on several levels. But eventually all the investigators will have to agree on one thing. I'm sure that the new powers-that-be, the future powers-that-be, will agree that a commanding officer, an old commie, wanted to get rid of the archive only to discover that someone else had beaten him to it. So what was he to do? He got frightened and took it out on the archivist who showed him the signed paperwork confirming that someone had taken delivery of the archive. When the officer realizes that it's all over for him – well, what does he do in this kind of pickle? Surely he won't swallow poison like a rat from a prefab high-rise? He won't overdose on sleeping pills – no, he will shoot himself, just like any professional officer anywhere in the world finding himself in this kind of trouble. He will shoot himself – that will be the reasoning of the bigwigs in the future. Another kind of investigation will be opened. That investigation is certain to be conducted by several – more than two – rival factions. Plenty of water will be muddied. Murky water. Troubled waters, like after an enormous flood. Regime change is always accompanied by an enormous flood. People fish in the muddy waters. Time will pass, many people will be replaced: many people will be sacked, others will be promoted. And only now – in the future, that is – will the archive that we have buried, only now will this archive rise from the dead! Yes, you heard right, Ondrej: the archive will rise from the dead. The deeper it will have sunk into oblivion, regardless of the kind of investigation that will have been conducted in the meantime, the deeper into the past the archive will have been plunged by the passage of time, the more refreshed it will be – mark my words: the archive will be like a giant waking up energized by a good night's sleep! The more people will try to forget it, the more powerful its presence will be. Because all these lads of ours, all those secret police hawks who once served under me, always stinking of the gym as if they hadn't bothered to shower after working out, all those who helped me bury the archive, will start to feel afraid! Do you understand? The archive will thrive on their fear. It will come to life! It will suddenly come alive! The archive will thrive on the fear of my young hawks, they will be scared that one of them might blab to the new powers-that-be, and so send the others to the cull. They won't be able to sleep, they'll be worried stiff about someone letting something slip to the new crème de la crème about the archive and the grave. There will be a winner and a king and the best they can hope for will be to be assigned menial work, if not sent behind bars. Behind bars! What an idealist you are, I thought to myself. Are you listening to me? I'm as sure as hell that none of my former hawks will blab about this to their wives and that all my young hawks will start watching one another, each will keep a watchful eye on all the others, like in a TV western. They will all know that they need not fear the old men, the ones who had once executed people there and stolen their foreign currency and gold. The only ones they'll suspect will be others in their own circle. They'll curse the old man – that is: me – , they'll damn me to hell for having got them mixed up in the burial of the archive and then slipping out by the back door, for having the last laugh by putting a bullet through my head, and leaving them here up to their necks in the soup, not just a hot soup, but a seething hot soup. And since they have learned their lesson, since my young hawks have learned to see anything and everything in terms of money, they will all believe that whoever breathes a word about the archive to the new powers-that-be is bound to be better off, so my young hawks will keep their eyes peeled to see whose wife has nicer clothes, who's gone on holiday and where, if anyone has a better kitchen, who has a new dishwasher, how come that so-and-so has moved to a new flat where the rent is six hundred crowns more – are you listening to me, Ostarok? And the colonel went on: The fear that they feel now will grow more and more horrendous. Their wives will browse mail order adverts and catalogues while I, their boss, the young hawks' boss, will slowly decompose in the soil and – if such a thing as the next world happens to exist – will be having one – well – hell of a laugh.

You've always hated them, I say to the colonel, I've known that from the start, so why do you want to commit suicide? Because of them? And he says: You know, I picked the biggest blockheads for this operation, for this burial of the archive. If you want me to put it more dramatically, to pigeonhole them more accurately, I would say that for this operation I picked the most evil men I could find.

Then, all of a sudden, the colonel asked me if I could, at this point, as he was about to die, picture the pit with the bones in every detail. I remember that the colonel asked me, rephrasing the question several times, who I thought the skeletons in the pit were. I didn't dare give him a straight answer and was reluctant to open my mouth. Germans? Partisans? Jews? Reich Germans? Ethnic Germans? Americans? Men who had served in the Hlinka Guard? Englishmen? Farmers from a nearby village? Who? Who? Come on, tell me, who? the colonel kept repeating, and I detected sad mockery in his voice. It increasingly seemed to me that the colonel was playing with me. Why did he have to remind me of that pit again? What kind of memento was it meant to be for me?

I took my time to answer. I felt that perhaps he expected me to say that I'd never seen anything like that before and never would again. Eventually I replied, somewhat uneasily, that I wasn't all that shocked by the pit because, as a matter of fact, I had seen things that were much worse. I told him about the time I went to see a colleague, the son of a professor of medicine, who had been refused admission to university and was working with me at the quarry. I've forgotten most of what the professor's son and I talked about that evening. What I did recall though, what had flashed through my mind several times before, was that while we were chatting, my eyes – only now and then to begin with, but almost continuously as the evening wore on – that my eyes kept wandering over to some uncanny little heads, heads as brown as smoked bacon rind, a handful of sculptures, four or five heads mounted on identical dark plinths. The hairless heads were no bigger than two fists put together, and they all seemed to look alike. That's probably what made me wonder, and made me feel increasingly certain, that they were just variations on the same sculpture. At the same time, however, I realized that I wasn't able to tell if the faces on these heads, displayed in the middle of a deep rectangular recess in a bureau, were meant to be the likenesses of men or women. I didn't know what it was about those heads that drew me to them. As I looked at them, I was gradually overcome by an irrational sense of unease. And throughout the melancholy time that I gazed at them, I experienced something, a kind of indefinable anxiety. It was a sensation akin to what I had felt in prison. You see, in prison you develop a kind of sixth sense that you can later never get rid of. Of course, I did notice early on that there was something disturbing about these likenesses, something beyond words. I might have found them disturbing from the minute I walked through the door, even before I had paid them proper attention. Every time I fixed my eyes on one of those heads, even if only for a few seconds, I was overcome by a strange, powerful sense that these statues, these heads crafted down to the finest detail, were basically not statues at all, and that if there was anything these heads could be compared to, it would be a kind of nonexistent photograph that had acquired three-dimensional form.

These are our patron saints, said my host, the son of the professor of medicine, when he noticed that I couldn't take my eyes off the heads on the sideboard. Casually, with a barely noticeable gesture, he pointed to the heads and continued, a little condescendingly: Don't they look noble? Proud – like Roman senators. Or emperors. – These are the shrunken heads of American Indians from Venezuela. The taxidermist: an unknown genius. It was my grandfather who brought them back from Venezuela. He donated the other heads to the Náprstek Museum. These few are the only ones he kept. When I was a boy, I used to line up the heads as an honorary guard in front of a castle I had made of building blocks. And look at me now! The quarry is where I've ended up! My grandfather said that the heads had been shrunk after they were hanged. See, there is a strangulation mark on every single head or, rather, neck. From the noose. I couldn't understand how anyone could bear to eat, drink, read newspapers and so on, in this room. So, this is the story I told the colonel, hoping that it might at least delay his suicide.

But despite having encountered evil in his professional capacity, despite being intimately familiar with a variety of techniques employed by evil, despite having spent most of his working life surrounded by evil, in defiance of all his professional experience, the colonel was a dreamer. He believed that when evil people form a group – no matter how large or small – sooner or later they end up killing each other, wiping each other out. That at the proverbial last minute they will fail to come to their senses and give an inch, however much they might like to, even if their own lives were at stake. But sometimes

I think that he wasn't a dreamer. And that evil is exactly as I have just described it.

The colonel claimed that evil has its own peculiar anatomy. Its own internal organism, and each kind of evil has a life of its own. With its own youth, virility, greying, ageing, and dying. No matter if the particular act of evil has been committed by someone with intelligence or a ruthless killer. I don't know how long I held forth to the colonel on the subject of the shrunken heads. Why should I have wondered about the bones in the pit, I, who had seen dead people's heads on a sideboard? And what difference was there between the son of a professor of medicine who failed to detect the presence of evil, and a warder at Valdice? I was horrified by those heads, despite having survived Valdice.

I think I gave the colonel a shorter version of the story, since he kept interrupting me. He insisted that he had yet to tell me the most important thing, which was that the mass grave contained nothing but fish. Deaf and dumb fish.

My dear colonel, please forgive me for telling you straight to your face, or rather, ear, I continued on the phone, you deliberately picked the crew for digging that mass grave from among murderers, from the firing squad, or what remained of it, in short, from those who had shot the people at the bottom of the pit, you, my dear colonel, literally hand-picked those old men as if using a pair of tweezers to peel postage stamps from an album. Perhaps you were aware of them long before you joined the secret police. You held your trump cards, your aces, close to your chest, right to the end. I asked him again and again why he had kept in his back pocket these six or seven old men, who had not yet found peace in death. Perhaps there were many more, but you picked the strongest of these old men, the best preserved ones, those who were still up to digging the pit, as they had done before. Even though, at the final stage, they had some help from those young hawks of yours. I remember pressing him further on whether he meant to stage the execution as a kind of reconstruction. Why hadn't he handed the case to the supreme court long ago? He said the reason was that, for one thing, he was afraid. For another, because he didn't trust the supreme court to re-open the case of some new, recently discovered mass grave, and third, because he was – well, had been – a family man. And fourth – the reason he had not revisited the case and showed it to the young hawks and to me earlier was that he was getting ready to bow out and to call the last shot. He added that he truly wanted to remind those murderers that fate would not forget about them, that there was someone out there who knew that they were ruthless killers, knew their names and their ID numbers, their addresses, the bank accounts their pensions went into, and so on. But why won't you ask me why I wanted the archive buried?

It may have been after uttering those words that the colonel shot himself. But I wouldn't put my head on the block for it. A bang at the other end of the line – as if something had exploded in my own head. Followed by silence. I went deaf. I couldn't hear the match being struck as I lit a cigarette. It occurred to me that I ought to report this to the police straight away, but at the same moment I was gripped by an unimaginable fear. A fear so powerful that it made me shake: I was trembling so much that my teeth started to chatter. I poured myself a brandy from a bottle I'd bought on my way to the hotel after saying goodbye to the colonel, and quickly downed a shot. I asked myself, I kept asking myself in my dazed state, somewhere on the boundary of consciousness and unconsciousness, whether I'd ever been this scared in Valdice but I could not, could not for the life of me, I could not, I confess, I really could not answer that question; there was just one thing that I realized with great clarity and still remember very clearly, and that is that I felt like an empty pair of wet pyjamas.

But my logical faculties were intact: I knew I couldn't call the police as they would barge in at once and start grilling me: How come that you, of all people, were the last person to talk to the colonel? Did you have a close relationship with him? What kind of relationship was it? The phrase 'delete where inapplicable' would have been of no use. What did you talk about just before he committed suicide? Did you have an argument? How come that it was you of all people who spoke to him on the phone, that it was you who were an eyewitness to the removal of the archive? What if you and the colonel had conspired to sell the archive to the intelligence services of a foreign power? And then you had a disagreement? Talk, talk, talk. We have experts who can make you talk. Yes: I was the first to experience the fear the colonel had spoken about.

I stayed at the hotel for three more days, three full days, I swear. I kept doing the rounds of doctors that my friends had recommended, my alleged friends, all of them obviously well-to-do hunting and shooting fellows, who owned cars the size of houses, I took glucose tests with and without a load (this procedure, along with being X-rayed from head to toe, took up one entire day), had an

ECG – it turned out that the left chamber of my heart had been weaker since birth. Had I known this in Valdice, the mere thought of it would have been the end of me. Then I subjected myself to the same battery of tests that I had recently undergone at the department of internal medicine: checks for bladder stones, cholesterol, bronchitis. These showed that my left kidney was weaker – hardly surprising given the idiosyncratic way I was taught to accustom myself to the cold. The urologist got hold of my stitched-up scrotum, the patched-up casing of my balls, pinching it beween his finger and thumb. What was that about? he asked. Valdice, I said. The doctor was a young man. He seemed a decent kind of chap. He stared at my empty sac, feeling it as if assessing material suitable for a winter coat, then asked: Valdice? What's that supposed to mean? Valdice? What's that?

All this time, all along, only one thing was on my mind, just one thing: had someone listened in on my telephone conversation with the colonel, even if he was the one who'd initiated the call? When would they come for me? Anxiously I waited for the night-time knock on the door. Every time I returned to the hotel, I looked around for men in twos. I would interrogate the receptionists, gawking at each one with a greedy male gaze, because eyes can't be castrated and they are great at play-acting. And since I was unable to pay them in kind with my balls the way a gardener can share his yield with others, I tipped them generously. Eventually I realized that no one had eavesdropped on our conversation, even though I'd used the hotel telephone. But how come they weren't monitoring phone calls from hotels? What do they eavesdrop on, if not hotels?

A few days later at the archives, I received his death notice in the post.

At first the colonel – whose real name I will never reveal, deliberately, as a matter of principle – seemed to be proven right. But only at first. Sure enough: the men who had taken part in the burial of the archive started to watch one another. To keep an eye on each other. After the end of the protracted investigation that, as expected, followed, and went on for several weeks. And now, even though the man we will continue calling the colonel was dead, he really got down to work. He was more present in the office, so to speak, than ever before. He embarked on a major clean-up, intent on polishing every doorhandle, catching up on every missed opportunity. People in the office were suddenly put through the grinder – the grinder, that's what it's called in the army, right? Everyone was investigating away like there was no tomorrow.

I forgot to mention a crucial thing: during the burial, the colonel managed to take some photos in secret with a tiny, western-made camera. Right after the burial he sent me the pictures in the post. I have them right here. I opened my desk drawer, took out the photos and spread them out for my guest to see.

Oh, so you don't want to see these pictures? One of the people in them is Major Šapes. He was the colonel's deputy. Nowadays a leading businessman. Surely you must know him. After all, he owns a department store in your town. I bet it's where you do your shopping. It has a grocery department on the ground floor and household goods upstairs. They sell everything you can think of, from vacuum cleaners, food processors and microwaves, to common-or-garden meat grinders. Why are you looking at me as if I had an epileptic fit coming on?

I have often thought – especially of late – about the colonel and his theory of evil. He was a modest man. Did you know that his favourite dish was Vitana packet soup? Of course you didn't. Vitana soup with plain rice and short noodles! He was no cheapskate though. One day he invited me to his house when he was pickling mushrooms. He'd brought a basketful of milk-caps from Orava. He was preparing the brine. He made me smell it and approve the taste with my tongue – as he put it. Our faces were wet with brine. Hot. Like after you've been holding your head over a camomile steam bath. I forget how the subject of evil came up again. He said the biggest drawback was that time always played into the hands of evil. Evil is very rarely caught red-handed and punished, like when honest cops are guarding the road between points X and Y on TV. No chance of a prompt police intervention like in the closing scene of a crime thriller, when the good cops descend from the sky *ex machina*! And he won me over when he said seriously, quite seriously: God never wastes a miracle, you know. That's not His way. You can't expect miracle-inflation from God.

He made his greatest mistake late in life: by getting married. But I've mentioned that before.

Sometimes he would make the following point: he started with it long before Communism collapsed in this country and went back to it again in the hour of his death. What he tried to convince me of, on several occasions, was that although he might not see as far as the very bottom of evil, the one and only thing that evil *per se* could be compared to was a particular kind of glass – the kind that is completely unbreakable, until something touches it at its critical point. A gentle tap at this point is enough to make the glass shatter. There is a kind of evil that holds together and stays as united and well-coordinated as a good ice hockey team. But then there comes a day when there's a tap and the genie is out of the bottle. It's all over. This is a law of nature that can't be observed in a test tube. Even if you have no conscience, nature will drive your body to the breaking point. And that's why, though innocent, you should never ask why it is that you have to endure so much pain, why you have to suffer the agonies of gout, what was the offence your parents and their parents before them committed to make you suffer so. You are the one who committed a crime inside them, even before you were born. Blood is a little bit like the tape in a tape recorder.

I have often thought that the colonel was wrong. Because fear did not sow division among his young hawks. Admittedly, at first they were quietly scared, but that lasted only a few hectic weeks. Later on, most of the men who had served under the colonel went into business. One bought a department store, another a garage, the third a dry cleaners', the fourth a hotel and the fifth something else, one man even became an undertaker. Now he owns two funeral parlours. He also produces those ceramic photographs you see on gravestones. Another has gone into street food, selling cheap snacks from a stall opposite the main station, and yet another runs a pest control firm. And there's the one who owns Morocco, the night club. That's also in your hometown. Not far from Šapes's department store. And here you have them all, our young hawks, in these photos, the old man had the pictures nicely blown up. Do you think the man whose boot crushed my balls has any regrets? He is now in charge of – forgive me if I laugh – humanizing the prison system.

Oh, how wrong the colonel had been to think that fear was the trump card! The colonel's former young hawks drove around in their Mercedeses, Fords, Mazdas and God knows what else. Fearless. Some of the young hawks would even drop in on me from time to time. To pick up some trout, if there was any to be had. One day I'd play host to one of them, the next day to another. They were good at boasting discreetly; they were no thugs. We would look each other straight in the eye, it was like a firm handshake. They never detected any trace of the photos of the burial in my eyes. We would drink and play cards. They kept testing me. To see if they could rely on me to treat them as before. Later I discovered that most of them were turning over millions. They have nearly all prospered. They all stick together – I'm talking as if this were still the case, though it's actually over. Admittedly, they created jobs for the unemployed, they even invited me to visit their businesses a few times. Everything was spotless. Impeccable service. As if – Mr Klementini – as if they were trying to send the message: let bygones be bygones, you were one of us out there, and look at us now: our smiling, clean-shaven faces, bespoke jackets, kindly eyes, friendly wives. Each year one of them would have me round for dinner on Christmas Eve – do you think I turned them down? Oh no, I accepted – and gladly! I hope I don't have to tell you why. I would spend a whole week choosing presents. We attended Midnight Mass together, like all good Catholics, and before going to church we had a few drinks and had our sour cabbage soup and carp. That's how things were with the young hawks. Only the other day one of them gave me this big book on world history. They send their children to the West every year – the kids should learn to speak foreign languages and the best way to live. That sort of thing.

Except that one day I heard that one of them, I think it was the man with the dry cleaning business, yes, that's who it was, got killed in a car accident. Suddenly dry cleaning was no longer lucrative. He was on the verge of bankruptcy. Apparently, the brakes in his car failed. And that same week another one ended up being stabbed to death in a bar. The Morocco.

And then, soon after the murder, suddenly, as if someone had waved a magic wand, the whole team of young hawks who used to scratch each other's back fell apart. The fellow who got stabbed must have been the key to the breakup. At least that's what I assume. The team literally fell apart. The only ones who remained here were Šapes and the owner of the Morocco.

One moved to Košice, two went to Zurich, several others to Lučenec, one ended up in South Africa – he bought some property on the cheap after the Poles began to leave. Another fetched up in Budapest. The gravediggers were the only ones who stayed in our neck of the woods. All the others send me postcards. At Christmas and at Easter, like the pharmacist. Postcards from their holidays. And holiday snaps too. Dads in straw hats with swelling bellies, innocent daddies, innocent wives, innocent children. Only the innocent old men are missing.

I have one more confession to make. After the colonel died, I started suffering from these strange fits. At first, they weren't real fits; I just felt dizzy and would lose my balance for a second or two. Black out. Initially I thought there was something wrong with my spine. One day it was so bad that an ambulance had to be called. I was extremely lucky that it happened when the head of the local hunting club was visiting me. Normally a quick-witted fellow. But on that occasion, he lost his nerve, as he freely admitted to me later – as I lay here on the floor, on these wooden boards. Later I did the rounds of the doctors. Eventually I was told in the hospital that it was epilepsy. The doctors were surprised that it manifested so late in life. That's why I have this German shepherd. My Regent. Except that I don't obey him. He's not an ordinary guard dog, the kind they have in institutions like this. Our pharmacist friend, our common acquaintance that is, who brought us together in this unusual way, is very good at getting hold of all sorts of journals. He has a wide range of interests. Just imagine, he discovered that in the English journal *Veterinary Record* a man called Andrew Edney claimed that dogs can feel or intuit that their owner might, or is about to, have an epileptic fit. So I got myself a German shepherd. A puppy. As you can see, he's turned into a strapping big fellow. And a wonderful young chap he is. Living proof that dogs, even those that haven't been specially trained and just happen to live with epilepsy sufferers, react in the right way. And quickly! Imagine! A dog – even an untrained one – can raise the alarm! He'll start jumping up and down. He'll bark! He'll charge at closed doors. He'll alert the neighbours.

Today, just before lunch, I was gripped by a feeling that Regent was concerned about something. Initially I ascribed it to the strange visitor we had earlier. The unknown woman. But after a while I had the increasingly strong impression that he was getting ready for something, on the lookout for something, because he just kept sniffing around. Eventually, he pushed the door open, bounded down to the ground floor, perhaps wanting to go out, but the main entrance door is kept locked. He often does this when he is restless. It's happened quite a few times that he rattled the door, or rather, the door handle, then ran upstairs and went to that door over there, then ran down the spiral staircase, tried the door handle and came back. That's what he does before I have a fit. Strange, isn't it? Forgive me if I laugh but it seems as if a fit was a kind of ghost who has to walk up the stairs, press down the doorhandle and open the door like a human being. I've given it a lot of thought. But there are times when all he does before I have a fit is give a brief bark. And he looks at me as he barks. When he is absolutely certain that I have taken notice of him, that I'm taking him seriously and paying him attention, that I regard him as a responsible creature, he runs over to the phone, jumps onto a chair and puts his paw down by the device. Funny that he has these two different ways of drawing my attention to an epileptic fit. But sometimes the whole spectacle proves completely unnecessary, and the fit doesn't materialise. But he is right most of the time.

Tell me, what is it about a dog's soul? How has the dog's soul learned to respond to an epileptic fit, of all things? Do you have an explanation for that, Mr Klementini? But now that I've raised the subject, let me stress one thing in particular: look at this well-chewed pencil, this blunt pencil. The first thing Regent would do if I fell on the floor during a fit is that he would take the pencil in his muzzle and push it between my teeth to prevent me from biting my tongue off. I taught him to do this myself and I'm very proud of that. If I collapsed on the floor right now, he would go and fetch the pencil straight away. But let's move on.

Now that I'm thinking about those young hawks – I don't seem to be able to get them out of my head – I have to admit that the colonel was right. The businessman who was stabbed to death in the bar... he really must have been the trigger, the most sensitive point in this particular instance of evil, tying all the young hawks together. And by dying he caused the unbreakable glass to shatter.

You're asking why I've brought up this stabbed man again? You've realised that I live in constant fear. And now, Mr Klementini, my fear has also frightened you.

But I haven't finished telling you the story of the colonel and his young hawks. Or of the colonel's findings and his speculation regarding the nature of evil. I mulled over his conclusions in Venice, the first time in my life I was able to travel abroad.

One evening the chairman of our cooperative farm – he is no longer chairman now – talked me into joining an organized trip to Padua and Venice. He said: I've heard that you speak German, we could use someone like you. The only problem was Regent. The chairman tried to persuade me not to treat him like a baby, he said that Regent would be happy to stay at his house, that they'd looked after him before.

We spent the first three days in Padua. The rest of the group headed for the shops. I gazed at shop windows crammed full of things and realized how easy it was to turn a person into an object. You won't believe it, but when we arrived in Venice, I started to feel like a prisoner again. Like a newly released prisoner, a prisoner freed a few days earlier, when I was first told that I could start working at the quarry. I was terrified of the loud clanking of the boats. Of the opulence of the houses. The beauty of the palazzi. I had never felt the presence of Valdice within me as powerfully as in Venice. What struck me most about Venice, what has left the greatest mark on me about it, was the smell of mould, the mustiness, the heavy stench of rotting water, the stink of the rats. I became scared of my own freedom. You won't believe it, but the absurd and unjustifiable feeling arose in me that I would have to return to Valdice one day. From Venice to Valdice, forever. I still don't understand it.

In Venice we were staying on an island. Away from the city. It was a small island. Some kind of a hostel. We would go back there only to sleep. But you can take my word for it, I couldn't for the life of me tell you what that island was called. I wish I remembered at least the number of the boat. If I knew the number of the boat line, I could find the rest. But then again, it doesn't matter what the island was called. Shopping in the mornings, beach in the afternoon. Horrendous. As the evening drew on, I would go out to the seafront just for a moment. I would gaze at the sea, at its majestic motion, swelling in and out. I don't know why but it reminded me of the operation of a loom. A weaving loom.

You know, ever since Valdice I wake up at around three in the morning. It's been like that for decades: I always wake up at that hour. At first it drove me to distraction. Especially in prison, that is. In those days I had no idea that it was ten to three. I would wake up at that precise moment, as if someone had poured a bucket of cold water over me. My eyes would pop open so wide that it hurt.

After that I'm never able to go back to sleep. In prison, of course, I used to be dreadfully exhausted. I kept tripping over; I'd fall asleep standing up and stagger every time I was kicked. You won't believe it, but insomnia is one of the things that helped me survive Valdice. You know why? Because I spent my days walking round as if in a dream. Reality was suppressed, no matter how horrible it was. I'm sure you know the sense that lingers after you've reached your destination when you've travelled by a fast train through night. The feeling of being dead tired, when everything around seems like a scene from a film that no longer has anything to do with you. As if you were looking at photos in someone else's album, that's how I felt in Valdice. And that feeling suddenly hit me with full force in Venice. I didn't enjoy anything. There was nothing that inspired my enthusiasm or admiration.

Throughout all the years in prison I had craved sleep, but at three o'clock this internal alarm clock would go off, the one I mentioned. Maybe this inability to sleep was a kind of protective foil or filter, perhaps it was the filter that prevented me from taking things fully in. If I'd had a chance to get a proper night's sleep, perhaps I'd have lost my mind. Not until after I was kicked out of prison following my accident was I able to get as much sleep as I wanted, yet I found that I would nevertheless wake up in the early hours, at ten to three – only now I had another option: I could have a really early night and feel quite rested by three in the morning.

And so in Venice, too, all I wanted to do was to be tucked up in bed by seven in the evening. Believe me, people don't appreciate the importance of a good bed. They don't appreciate decent bedlinen. I don't know why, but in Venice, before going to sleep, I often thought of a fellow inmate who was able to dream on demand. To prescribe his own dreams. What kind of dream he should have and what it should be about. In one of his favourite dreams-on-demand he would be working in a garden. He had never had a garden. In another favourite dream, he would be walking up and down the deck of a big ship, sailing the high seas – the image of the ship and the sea came from a film he had seen.

A proper prison will set your timetable for years to come, long after you're out. And even though you're out, a time machine from hell keeps ticking inside you. It keeps pointing out this and that. And although in Venice I was worried that I might get a fit, even an ordinary epileptic fit can be quite clever. Imagine – apart from two or three occasions – I have never had a fit outside my home. I have often thought of Regent. You see, I have browsed the museum catalogues and monographs I bought in Padua on our first or second day, when I still thought that I ought to go and visit one of those galleries now that, after all those years, I had a chance to see something as a free man. But you won't believe it. I was so dazzled by Venice that it felt like staring into the headlights while being slapped across the face by the men of the secret police.

What? What did you say? That I'm suffering from cabin fever? – Yes, I've heard of cabin fever. Well, you've managed to spend quite a while with me in this cabin that nobody visits anymore.

What? The only thing you were interested in was your parents' case? Everything I've told you relates to the case of somebody's parents, yours included. Don't fool yourself that just because you're one generation younger than me you're better off. What a fool I've been! I should have listened to the pharmacist and the woman who came to see me this morning to warn me about you! That woman must have known more about you than Vrtiak did until recently! What a shame you didn't meet her. But perhaps you were the judge at her trial?...

You may not yet be aware, but I have shut the door of this cabin on you. From now on, you'll be stuck here with me forever.

p. 22   Czechoslovak First Republic – Czechoslovakia in the period 1918–1938, as commonly referred to in the country.

p. 23   Valdice – the oldest, largest and harshest prison in the Czech Republic, located northeast of Prague in a former Carthusian monastery built in the seventeenth century, converted into a prison in the 1850s.

p. 26   Voice of America – state-owned international radio broadcaster of the United States of America, a prohibited yet favourite source of free information in Cold War Czechoslovakia.

p. 31   Novotný – Antonín Novotný (1904–1975) Czech politician, First Secretary of the Czechoslovak Communist Party (1953–1968), later also President of Czechoslovakia (1957–1968). He withdrew from political life after being ousted in 1968. Following Soviet leader Nikita Khrushchev's example he declared a broad amnesty for political prisoners in 1960.

p. 34   Gottwald – Klement Gottwald (1896–1953) Czechoslovak politician, first communist President of Czechoslovakia (1948–1953).

p. 36   slivovitz – plum brandy

p. 36   Ferko Urbánek (1858–1934) – Slovak playwright whose plays are frequently staged by amateur theatre companies.

p. 37   Bukharin, Kamenev, Zinoviev, Trotsky – Nikolai Bukharin (1888–1938), Lev Kamenev (1883–1936) and Grigory Zinoviev (1883–1936) were high-ranking Soviet Communists who took part in the Bolshevik Revolution, were arrested on Stalin's orders during the Great Purge 1936 and subsequently executed; Leon Trotsky (1879–1940) was expelled from the Soviet Union in 1929 and assassinated in Mexico.

p. 38   Section III – the most notorious part of Valdice prison

p. 42   Twentieth Communist Party Congress of the USSR – held in February 1954, at which Nikita Khrushchev denounced Stalin's personality cult.

p. 43   Slánský – Rudolf Slánský, (1901–1952) Czechoslovak communist politician, one of the organizers and later the victim, of the communist terror in the late 1940s and early 1950s; sentenced to death and executed in the 1952 show trials.

p. 44 Nosek – Václav Nosek (1892–1955), Czech politician, leading Communist party figure, Czechoslovakia's Minister of the Interior from 1945 to 1953.

p. 45 Clementis – Vladimír Clementis (1902–1952) Slovak politician, writer, translator, leftist intellectual, diplomat; in the biggest show trial of the 1950s he was sentenced to death and executed alongside Rudolf Slánský and others.

p. 48 Široký – Viliam Široký (1902–1971) Slovak politician, functionary in the Czechoslovak Communist Party, representative of the period of the cult of personality, initiator of political trials in Slovakia.

p. 48 "When the Warsaw Pact barged into the country" – reference to the Soviet-led invasion of Czechoslovakia in August 1968.

p. 50 "The minister, the chubby minister, tumbles out of a narrow window..." – reference to Jan Masaryk (1886–1948), son of the founder of Czechoslovakia, Thomas Garrigue Masaryk, who served as the country's Minister of Foreign Affairs from 1940 to 1948 and died by falling or being pushed out of a window.

p. 50 Bacílek – Karol Bacílek (1896–1974) a high-ranking Communist party official and politician who served as the First Secretary of the Communist Party of Slovakia before being deposed in 1963 and replaced by Alexander Dubček.

p. 54 Velvet Revolution – the popular uprising that overthrew the Communist regime in Czechoslovakia, known in Slovakia as the Tender Revolution.

p. 54 Havel – Václav Havel, Czech playwright, dissident, political prisoner and later the last President of Czechoslovakia and first President of the Czech Republic

p. 56 VPN badge – worn by members or supporters of Verejnosť proti násiliu (Public Against Violence), the movement, and later party, which in November 1989 led the Velvet Revolution in Slovakia.

p. 57 borovička – Slovak spirit similar to gin

JOHANIDES'S NOUGHTS AND BOSSES
ROBERT B. PYNSENT

SHAPES IN JOHANIDES'S NOVEL

The opening one-sentence-paragraph of Ján Johanides's (1934–2008) *But Crime Does Punish* (Trestajúci zločin, 1995) constitutes a portrait of the narrator's character, but also the way memory works and thereby introduces us to the geometrical shapes that indicate not only the author's narrative method and art-history training, but also to the principal events in the narrator's life, events that make the most of that 'bundle of sensations' that shapes his identity. For most of the narrator's life after he was released from prison he has been employed by the Ministry of the Interior, in this case by the secret police, as guardian of a castle or old manor that contained the top-secret files of the police and of the (show) trials which they instigated. For the general public, the building serves as a museum of Slovak flora and fauna, that is dried flowers and stuffed animals, ironic metaphors for the files, and the fates of the people whose cases they contain. This guardian is a bureaucrat and his 'may I?' (*dovolíte?*) might indicate politeness, but the adverb attached to it, *úslužne* (obligingly) suggests a degree of servility associated with the bureaucrats of Habsburg or post-Habsburg states. Mind you, he lacks completely the arrogance that conventionally melded with that servility.

The first geometric shape to arise in the book is the narrator's route in the train corridor, which is a loop or oblong, for he never reaches the back. Memory is just such a loop from present to past back to present – and in this brief novel a variety of other loops hang from the straight sides of the oblong, like safety pins of different sizes.

The shape also alludes to the shape of pre-Second-World-War Czechoslovakia, a malformed oblong, and the novel does give an outline of Czechoslovakia's history by depicting its beginnings on the Eastern Front during the First World War, not explicitly stated but an allusion evident to any Czechoslovak reader (Czechs and Slovaks deserting to the other side and joining up with compatriots who live in Russia and subsequently with P.O.W.s to form legions labelled the Czechoslovak Army in Russia [Československá armáda na Rusi]). Trench warfare resides in the memory of the narrator's grandfather. As far as the understanding of Johanides's ironic and consistently anti-sentimental method is concerned, in the trench celebration of Christmas in 1914 and 1915 there were three days of cease-fire when both the Western and the Orthodox Church celebrated Christmas Eve, Christmas Day and the Feast of St. Stephen. Soon after the 1915 cease-fire the narrator's grandfather sees one of the men bayonetting a Russian soldier they had been friendly with and delighting in winding the Russian's intestines round his bayonet. The reader notes the circularity of this movement of sheer sadism – a sadism that prefigures the portrait of the atmosphere of life dominated by the Soviet-style Communist Party from 1945 (not just from February 1948) until 1989. Such irony is a device to smother bitterness.

It takes time before the reader learns the uncomfortable narrator's name, which is important for the understanding of the novel and, indeed, for some understanding of the first paragraph, and of Johanides's apparently playful irony. The guardian of the files bears the name Ondrej Ostarok; *ostarok* is a stunted tree or man.[1] So the emasculated Ostarok contrasts with his Christian name, Ondrej [Andrew], meaning 'manly'.[2] Now we have two more loops: Ondrej Ostarok's initials OO could indicate the two testicles Ostarok lost in Valdice, perhaps at the hands or feet of the frustrated homosexual warder who just cannot get his penis into Ostarok's anus. On the other hand, crushing testicles was a fairly common form of torture in Stalinist prisons, known sarcastically by ex-prisoners and secret policemen as *rajský protlak*, 'tomato puree'. Johanides was not at all anti-homosexual; in the

1   The other meaning, a precautious child, visually related, is irrelevant.
2   Johanides could be also playing with the fact that St Andrew, the first called (*i.e.* first disciple of Jesus) was the patron saint of Russia, and indeed in a medieval tradition, spread the gospel in parts of south Russia as well as Asia Minor. I think irrelevant to Johanides, though one can never be certain, that in a very late medieval tradition Andrew was the first bishop of Byzantium and was crucified on a saltire – though a saltire could be associated in terms of pain with Ostarok's emasculation in prison in Valdice, Bohemia.

1940s and 1950s homosexuals who had previously worked for the SD (Sicherheitsdienst) in setting up flats and male prostitutes for homosexual German soldiers were employed by the Czechoslovak secret police as informers in prisons and labour camps. Johanides is playing on Latin *testes* meaning not only 'testicle' but primarily a 'witness' or 'someone who testifies to a fact'. Certainly, Ostarok is, probably above all, a witness – a witness to the horrors the Stalinists imposed on Czechoslovaks, and to the fact that the 1960s was actually largely eyewash.

Upon leaving prison in a mid-1960s amnesty, Ostarok is given a job in a quarry, the first of two pits (empty structures that could also be represented as Os) that appear in the novel. In the quarry, although he is never put in charge of any explosives, he would be blamed for an inevitable (because of the poor safety standards under Soviet-style Communist regimes) and fatal accident involving one, which would lead to him being imprisoned again. The second pit contains the remains of people shot in 1944, perhaps Germans during the Slovak National Uprising, perhaps Slovaks shot by Germans, perhaps Jews shot by Slovaks or Germans. A secret police colonel organizes the exhumation and gathers the people who had been involved in the mass shooting to do the digging. The colonel takes Ostarok to witness the casting of all the secret files into the pit over these remains, the quickliming of the files, and the re-filling of the pit. In fact, Ostarok becomes the sole non-criminal, non-police witness. This episode actually relieves the participants of the sense of guilt for the shooting, for they had been dreading being punished for the original killing for forty-four years. The secret police employees who take the files to the pit, however, appear gradually to kill off each other or themselves. Eventually, having helped everyone he believes he can, the colonel commits suicide. To a degree, Ostarok's dog, Regent, takes over the colonel's role. Only after the colonel's death does Ostarok start having epileptic seizures about which Regent warns him – hence the dog's name.

This unnamed secret-police colonel is probably the only wholly good character in *But Crime Does Punish*: there is nothing bad in Ostarok, but he as an *ostarok*, stunted by his castration, is powerless, except as the warder of the files, but that is just a bureaucratic function. In the end, he does manifest goodness in the framework story: a man called Klementini had lost both parents who were executed in the 1950s, his father largely on the basis of the testimony of his wife, who had been beaten until she agreed to state what the secret police wanted to hear, in her husband's trial. Ostarok decides not to tell Klementini, for in his case, knowledge of the truth would be more painful than ignorance. I assume that the name Klementini indicates Latin *clementia*, here the clemency of being granted ignorance. Here the colonel posthumously reveals his influence on Ostarok, for the colonel understands that sometimes forgetting is far more humane than remembering. Forgetting is a precious gift. The colonel's teachings (for he is a teacher and well nigh a god figure) sometimes match what Ostarok had painfully learned in prison. After all, learning to forget often amounts to much the same thing as learning not to see: 'I refused to believe my own eyes: that's something you learn inside. I looked away. The reflex that my head had cultivated for years was still in perfect working order.' (*Trestajúci zločin*, 24–25). Here, however, it is Ostarok the bureaucrat's thinking somewhat mitigating the colonel's.

That brings the reader back to the second pit, for at the time Johanides was writing, a different, even larger, pit was in the news – a pit that had been investigated in 1947, but the whole affair was covered up and hardly ever even talked about during the reign of the Communist Party. This was the pit in Švédské šance near Přerov in Moravia, that is, not at all far from Slovakia.[3] The whole affair was entirely Slovak with a little Soviet support. The gang leader was an officer of the infamous OBZ (*Obranné spravodajstvo*, defence intelligence) from Petržalka. His name was Karol Pazúr. A train full of Carpathian Germans, mainly old people, women and children, were returning from the Sudetengau whither they had been sent for safety by the German authorities, as the Red Army advance continued. They were on their way

3   The fact that the mass shooting here took place in June 1945, and not in 1944, is probably irrelevant.

back home, mostly to or via the town of Dobšiná, once the world centre for cobalt mining but now pretty poor; on 1930s postcards of Dobšiná one notices that the majority of the population is barefoot. Pazúr told the Czechoslovak authorities that these innocent people were war criminals, Nazis and SS; and with permission, not from the Czechoslovaks, but from a Soviet officer, he emptied the train and marched the Carpathian Germans to a field where they were all shot by Pazúr and his friends. Pazúr ordered the Czech authorities to provide men to dig a pit for the 246 corpses. During the war Pazúr had briefly been a member of the HG (Hlinkova garda, equivalent of the German SA); before the completion of the Communist takeover in February 1948, he was tried and given a long gaol sentence, but soon he re-appeared as a member of the secret police, decked out in numerous medals. He became a heavy drinker and died before the Changes of 1989–90. A memorial to the murder victims was erected in 1993, while Johanides was writing *But Crime Does Punish.*[4]

SURVEY OF JOHANIDES'S WORKS

Ján Johanides published his first work *Súkromie* (Privacy), a collection of five short stories, in 1963. He belonged to what was labelled the Generation of '56, those writers who made their first literary appearance in the journal *Mladá kultúra* (Young culture) in 1956 or 1957. He remained mainly a writer of prose fiction though he did publish a play, and a collection of essays. He went up to Bratislava University in 1954, began but never finished, reading aesthetics and art history. From the Warsaw Pact intervention in 1968 onwards he lived outside Bratislava and, like most decent Slovak writers, could not publish again until the mid- to late 1970s (Czech writers mostly had to wait until 1989 or 1990, I suspect because of the entirely different attitude to literary culture in Slovakia from that of the Bohemian lands; the Slovak Minister

4 For the history of the mass murder, its commemorations and so forth, see František Hýbl's *Tragédie na Švédských šancích v červnu 1945* [1995] and his *Krvavá noc na Švédských šancích nedaleko Přerova 18. a 19. června 1945* [second expanded edition 2018].

of Culture was a pretty good poet, Miroslav Válek, but drink over-took him.) Johanides's *Súkromie* manifests the direct influence of the nouveau romancier Michel Butor, and Existentialism of the Camus brand also marks his subsequent two works. In the first story, 'Nerozhodný' (Indecisive), Johanides is bold for the times in his portrayal of Slovak treatment of the Jewish physician Em-bler (just the letter *l* away from *ember*, the Hungarian for human being); his 'Christian' Slovak colleagues allow him to be arrested and sent off to, the reader assumes, a death camp. The doctor who coldly suggests Embler's replacement had been his closest friend. The Slovak war-time puppet state was the first country voluntari-ly to send Jews to Auschwitz and to pay the Reichsbahn for taking them there. That is the shame Johanides is writing about in this episode.[5] In *Nerozhodný*, Johanides introduces his possibly most frequent motif throughout his works, guilt, which he here links up with notions of freedom and indeed, prison. Blood is a strong motif in this story, as it is in many, if not most, subsequent stories and novels – including *But Crime Does Punish*. Here, too, the main character is a *vous* as in Butor, who had been a works doctor in a quarry. And Johanides's second work is *Podstata kameňolomu* (The Essence of the Quarry, 1965), a novel, a part of which is presented in the form of a drama, with stage-directions and so forth. Here the quarry is somewhere the main character visits, somewhere that has something like a cryptamnesic role in his life: it causes changes first in his actions, but soon also in his per-sonality – to such a degree that the reader cannot be quite sure whether the main character is always the same man. Perhaps he looks forward to Ondrej Ostarok in that he is a character in flux. The third work of the 1960s is *Nie* (No, 1966), which makes for

5   In the late 1980s I published an article on the Jews in contemporary Slovak literature; soon afterwards the Slovak Union of Writers asked me for a list of the papers I had written about Slovak literature; when that list was published, the article on the Shoah was omitted. Soviet-style Communists did not like mentions of the subject; literature should portray the glories of the given country's fight against 'fascism' (i.e. Nazism, Fascism, Falangism and the rest) or 'imperialism' (the Western occupation of new territory). Still today, Putin's invasions of Ukraine in 2014 and 2022 are not imperialist, of course.

the apex of the sensualism that marks Johanides's early works and perhaps returns only with what some consider his greatest work, the historical novel *Marek koniar a uhorský pápež* (Marek the Master of Horse and the Hungarian Pope, 1983). In *Nie* guilt appears, in true Existentialist manner, to form an essential part of the human condition and here perhaps in particular of women, for here *žena* L ('the woman L'), that is 'Elle' states that she has normal sensations of guilt and that such a sensation of guilt is not at all explicable. This sensation seems to be associated with her puberty and the smell of blood coming from the slaughter-house she had lived near, and indeed the blood of an escaped calf that is killed in her garden. The sensualism is part of the vitalism evinced in this novel: the world of Nature is such a wonderful place, completely wasted on such horrific creatures as human beings. 'Elle' comes to the conclusion that life can only consist in frustrated life: 'in life, life itself is unrealisable' (*Nie*, p. 24). In the end, however, 'Elle' becomes something of a flirt, which she claims she had done out of despair at life. In *Nie*, all life appears to be associated with sexuality and the blood-soaked red rose of Original Sin. Sexual intercourse can destroy intellectual creativity by invading someone's inner privacy. The very movements of the erotic, clasping and embracing, make for a prison. *Nie* ends with a lengthy passage on the godless world and here the writer who had accompanied 'Elle', on looking down onto the godlessness, suddenly stoops 'as if he had received a blow to his testicles; he grabs them and it looks as if the whole town had just kicked him in the genitals' (*Nie*, p. 78). Johanides was a Christian.

After *Nie*, his first book was *Nepriznané vrany* (Unacknowledged Crows, 1978) which concerns on one level the pollution caused by an artificial fertiliser factory, on another the problem of writing altogether, but chiefly what writing literature for the (common) people is, can or should be. It is still no conventional novel, but a discussion interspersed with anecdotes, painterly descriptions, and impressions. Šaňo, a friend of the journalist first-person narrator, tells him what to write for the people, a song about a savings book – which looks forward to Johanides's next book, but also ironically states that all the 'people' of post-1969 Normalization are concerned with is money, the material. Later, writing for the people is associated with trash like the Angélique series. *Balada o vkladnej knižke* (The Ballad of a Savings Book, 1979) again concerns itself with money-lust, greed, selfishness, by the end of the 1970s, the dominant social atmosphere of Communist-led Czechoslovakia as well as the West, though that becomes worse in the 1980s. Johanides is not pessimistic here, even though he reveals himself as something of a biological determinist (a passing phase in his thinking). Perhaps interesting for Johanides as a whole in this somewhat dour novella is the episode of the woman whom a palmist had told she would die in an air-raid. She tried to avoid that fate by burning away the lines on her palm with acid. And indeed, she does not die exactly as expected, but because while opening a garage door to give lover and friends shelter, a lump of concrete falls on her. Only with his third Normalization novel, *Marek koniar*, does Johanides return to his old self. Set in the early sixteenth century, it is a lively attempt to present the psychology of a few characters of different social backgrounds, including the peasant Hungarian Bakócz who is hoping to be elected pope. This complex novel re-introduces the reader to Johanides's recurrent search for spiritual meaning in physical actions – and here that is often rendered by the esoteric, treated as a characteristic of the times portrayed. The story itself is more or less irrelevant. The early sixteenth century certainly has some similarity with the money-minded 1980s: it is a rough, power-lusting, fickle period. Of course, Johanides has plenty of form here – thus a torturer friend of Marek's bears the name Moczart. Marek has also learned, as a sceptic and a sensitive man, that sincerity is a luxury that often does more harm than good and that looks forward to the lessons learned, often from the colonel, by Ostarok in *But Crime Does Punish*. In the next novel dedication which concerns the Second World War he informs us that the family of his Protestant mother had been shot at the Babi Yar by Kyiv in 1941, possibly the greatest atrocity in the antisemitic genocide. The title of the novel *Slony v Mauthausene* (Elephants in Mauthausen, 1985), alludes, amongst other minor elephant scenes, to one that comes latish in the novel, when a teenager persuades some small children to play at being elephants when they have been ordered to enter a mobile gas chamber. Mauthausen had an infamous quarry where many an inmate was beaten to death or thrown to his/her death. Only one person from the family of Johanides's father survived Mauthausen. I suppose there can be no doubt that this accounts for the frequency with which quarries and other pits appear in Johanides's fiction. The framework of the novel concerns a former Dutch inmate's visiting the Slovak former inmate, the Communist writer Ferdinand Holenyšt (F. absolutely nothing). It is unusual for Johanides to show the ignorance he does by giving the Dutchman a Christian name he couldn't have been given as a child before 1945 and which was then most common amongst West Indians; he is Winston van Mease, a petty nobleman on top of it. In fact, Johanides appears in this novel to be self-consciously composing a mythology of the ordinary Slovak workers' experience of the Second World War. It is an entirely political or politicized novel and that does not suit the author's creative mentality. It is possible that someone had put pressure on him, but more likely that he wanted to create a memorial of his own to his parents' families and found that he could not be creatively political but that he needed to have a try. Amongst the Scandinavians remembered in the camp one hears the name Goorg Brandes, which is either just a feeble joke or a device to tell the reader he is not writing this willingly. On the other hand, it does give him the chance to say something about Jews and antisemitism, most effectively through the figure of the Orthodox Jew Rigelhaupt. A particularly grim picture is that of a Slovak mother of eleven children and passion play actress, who on the very spot where Rigelhaupt had had his shop, enthusiastically plays the role of inspector of Jewish vaginas, just in case, of course, the women should be hiding gold there. On the whole, however, any reader will be shocked by the number of Czechoslovak Communist establishment clichés to be found in *Slony v Mauthausene*. Johanides is extraordinarily (in every meaning of the word) unoriginal here, except by mistake. For example, we hear of a Punjabi who was mistakenly imprisoned for twenty-eight years in a British concentration camp in Rhodesia, even 'Rhodesia' is wrong for the period.

The author's next work, a collection of four short stories, *Pochovávanie brata* (Burying a Brother, 1987), is even weaker in achieving the author's normal coherent inventiveness than *Slony v Mauthausene*. Johanides manifests in *Pochovávanie brata* his interest in the self as myth, that also reflects the time of writing that witnessed the fashionable mythology of losing or finding one's self, and of everyone having a 'real self'. What is new in Johanides here is the picture of Party-led obliteration of communal memory by bulldozing cemeteries. In *But Crime Does Punish* that will be reconfigured in the scene in which a slightly drunk young Ostarok with Vrtiak and a young woman who yells at the two secret policemen who had been following them that they had done this to Ostarok. Thus Ostarok learns that his scrotum has become a state secret. That has nothing to do with the gift of selective oblivion. In *Pochovávanie brata* he touches on the Shoah again by describing the aryanization of the Silberstein ironmongery. Oppression, of course, associates both forms of totalitarianism, and thus living in the 'socialist' brands of pre-fabricated panel blocks of flats, thus being forced to accept 'socialist norms' leads to universal turpitude. Similarly, the Second World War can become the source of free alcohol for some old-age pensioners. A group of men in a pub invites a Communist old-age pensioner over to their table; they know that once he gets going about the war, he will pay for their gin: working-class cynicism. Still, Johanides's playful literary experimenting and narrative inventiveness has almost completely disappeared in this collection.

His next work, the novel *Najsmutnejšia oravská balada* (The Saddest Ballad of Orava) appeared in the year of the Bratislava Easter (or Candle) demonstrations and one or two other authors published works which could not have been published before: 1988.[6] Orava is the northern county where Johanides had been born. Though the narrative framework is set in 1986, most of the

6 See one of them translated into English by Charles Sabatos: Pavel Vilikovský's *Ever Green Is...*, published by Northwestern University Press, 2002.

novel concerns the history of the county and the family, Brecher/
Brechár, from the Napoleonic wars, and then, particularly in the
1840s. The Brechár family had come to Orava in *c.* 1846 from
Dresden. In *Najsmutnejšia oravská balada* Johanides seeks to evoke
a series of atmospheres, not unlike Umberto Eco, or two earlier
Slovak writers, Dobroslav Chrobák (1907–1951) and Rudolf Jašík
(1919–1960). The novel opens with a portrayal of melancholy (later
sometimes labelled 'pain') which constitutes one of its themes. By
means of the somewhat unsightly couple, Poldo (130 kg, 170 cm;
plus his monthly migraine) and his (future) wife, Betka (about
30 kg lighter); the people around them consider their feelings for
each other a deformation of human behaviour. Poldo and Betka
are not Jews, but the community's approach to them intentionally
serves as a statement on antisemitism: they 'began to understand
what physiological hatred was, when the people in the Karlova
Ves restaurant abused them as Jews. Poldo and Betka look at
each other and burst into a Lutheran guffaw.' (p. 12). Here this is
associated with the theme of melancholy and its causes, where the
novel has set out to discover the melancholy in the beauty of the
Orava county in which it is domiciled in the murder of two Brechár
brothers in the Brechár mill, and in the jackboots of the Brechár
who claims to hate populist Slovak and Hlinka Guard nationalisms.
This Brechár has been an Agrarian, later a Democrat (a short-
lived, post-Second World War political party) who liked reading
Westerns – as well as a courageous partisan and then fighter in
the Slovak National Uprising. One sees in him how Johanides is
destroying the imposed simple black-and-white understanding of
Communist Party historiography. Still, this Brechár ends up a not
insignificant functionary in the Regional National Committee –
still a 'strange, wild, inconsistent, sick man' (p. 21), who after
February 1948 began cursing the Democrats for whom he had
voted, and by 1951 he was being driven about in one of the
standard Party would-be luxurious Tatras. His mother and his
aunts had all been prostitutes, which Johanides derives from the
well-established incest in upper Orava, where fathers or brothers
introduced their daughters or sisters to sexual intercourse. His
former prostitute mother and aunts had learned Czech from their

pimp's wife Jarmila[7] and later his mother and aunts learn German and Hungarian as befits Slovak whores. Brechár's two aunts love reading another Czech, Quido Maria Vyskočil (1881–1969), a writer of trite, cliché-riddled verse and prose that was only rarely of more literary interest than the verse. Poldo's father eventually dies of liver failure, a rather Slovak death, one that Johanides's own son would, exhibiting considerable self-sacrifice, endeavour to prevent his father meeting. I do not know whether the following is – was – a common practice; when Poldo's father dies, slices of bacon had been placed around his thighs, arms and belly to diminish the stench of decomposition. That is narrated in a combination of verisimilitude and comedy that makes for earthy morbidity – especially since it took three kg of lemons, a none too common fruit in Communist Slovakia. This history of Slovakia is told largely in a series of monologues, which conceptually does look forward to *But Crime Does Punish*. Like Vilikovský, Johanides does in *Najsmutnejšia oravská balada* break the bounds of Communist respectability – of which a passage on the physical and psychological growth of Communist bureaucrats in the 1960s and 1970s and their children's relationship to them represent a statement on contemporaneous hypocrisy: 'The young showed respect for their fathers and were proud of them, even though they were secretly ashamed of them' (p. 61). The corruption of party bosses also forms a theme – but that we have already seen in the father of Slovak party-critical high literature, Alfonz Bednár (1914–1989). Johanides goes a little further in that he makes a collective farm boss not only a former member of the Hlinka Guard, but also the aryaniser of a three-storey draper's shop, and a secret policeman who has been dismissed from the service for punching Roman Catholic priests in Ružomberok prison. Poldo is far more interested in the writings of Johannes Reuchlin, a neo-Platonist of the Cabalist mode (1455–1522) than he is in the politics of his own age. Poldo, however, considers the Renaissance a vulgar age, an age vulgarised by decorativeness –

7 Name perhaps an ironic allusion to the bandit's beloved of the Czech K.H. Mácha's narrative poem, who had been introduced to coitus by her beloved's father, whom his beloved consequently kills.

and where the majority of the population 'longed for fairgrounds and chewing gum' (p. 144). The novel ends in blood when one of the narrator Poldo's boyhood friends, Filip, is stabbed by a thug with a cheap flick-knife; if anyone were to be stabbed, Poldo maintains, it should have been Poldo himself. But Filip had to be killed because, when in gaol, he had stolen blankets from fellow-prisoners.

In the year the Red Army left the Czecho-Slovak Federal Republic and the Soviet Union began to disintegrate, Johanides's first work published in post-Communist Slovakia was *Previesť cez most. Rúcha veleby pre chvíle tiesne* (Taking Across the Bridge. Grand Robes for Moments of Distress, 1991). The initial part of the title refers to Kristína who gives the narrator Ján Stefanides a lift to the town of Levice; when he is getting out, Kristína thanks him for taking her across the bridge over a precipice, that is, between non-being and being. Stefanides comes close to being something of a double of the author: he is an art historian. His wife Milica is stable, kind and practical like Johanides's wife but does not have asthma like her (hence their living in the pre-fab panel block in a town outside Bratislava). Stefanides has an essential quality of previous characters in Johanides's works; his father had been a prisoner in Mauthausen. *Previesť cez most* concerns various states of consciousness, in particular that state of non-being created by severe mental sickness. The setting appears to be 1979 and the framework action concerns two aspects of Stefanides's life. First, the elderly former Baťa leather expert, and art collector, Dušnic's telephone calls to and meetings with Stefanides; Dušnic, an anchor for Stefanides, shows sincere gratitude when Stefanides cancels his trip to Italy, partly to see his noble former mistress Fiducia Maria Gloria ze Šternberka. Secondly, two other characters, Lojzo and Pusina visit Stefanides in order to borrow a large sum of money; Stefanides agrees to it, but practical Milica is furious. On the way back to Levice Pusina suddenly goes out of her mind and smashes up a station restaurant. She is taken to a mental hospital, locally referred to as Mefistopolis and Lojzo rings Stefanides to ask him to come to the hospital to try to settle Pusina down with the help of a consultant, but he finds her entirely mad, apparently incurably so. This is only one of several episodes centered on confinement in Mefistopolis or another mental hospital, which serves as a parallel to, if not a straight metaphor of, the theme of disintegration, social and 'national' that in the course of the novel is most clearly noted during the Second World War and the post-1969 Normalization. In all periods the name Stefanides unites the Czechs with the Slovaks. A wartime German officer tells the young Stefanides that he is a noble, which he is not, and that he knows his name reveals that his family had come as Protestant exiles to Upper Hungary (= more or less today's Slovakia) from Bohemia after the Roman Catholic army had defeated the Protestant at the Battle of the White Mountain (1620). Not only because Stefanides is an art dealer (and Johanides an aesthetician and art historian), may one call *Preniesť cez most* an aesthetic novel. One day, in a room many miles away from a factory the Germans are bombing, a Stradivarius cracks. A thing of true beauty has a sensitivity that is almost supernatural: that is the most evident testimony to that fact, and is the clearest of the points in which we understand that, subtly, Johanides has written a novel mainly about beauty – and the destruction of beauty. Greed, Nazism, Soviet-style socialism, and the drunken states of most of the characters, at least on frequent occasions, destroys beauty. Another example is the morbid bureaucratization of cremation that Johanides satirizes in one of his pieces on Normalization; the ashes of all those cremated will be poured into plastic envelopes and appended to their personal files; the following is spoken by the official elogist:

The crematorium will give the ashes-filled envelopes to individual employee departments, where the ashes of the dead will be allotted a file number and attached to their quondam personnel file and listed together with the personnel file as an inseparable component of the notional basic stock of employees. In a particular paragraph of her speech the elogist pointed out to the deceased's family that they would be permitted to borrow the ashes from the firm or institution on confirmation that they are for a family memorial celebration after completing a form, on which must first be entered the date of the memorial act, agreed by the leadership of the firm.

Every firm must earmark one member of the typing pool for these duties. (p. 28)

Another example of the destruction of solemnity, beauty is a picture of blood in a wrecked garden, a hyperbolic version of what we saw in *Nie*, where the sensuality of the *Nie* scene has become the arbitrary violence of early twentieth-century war (or, for today, of Russian war in Ukraine). At the Battle of Austerlitz, one of Fiducia's antecedents, Caspar von Sternberg, has blood and corpses in his botanical garden reaching the upper branches of his redcurrant plants and no one except the Count would know how many other plants were thus mangled. Pusina's consultant dehumanizes not his patients but those outside the hospital, by labelling them with names of mental sicknesses, thus 'an asthenic, a cathetic angel' or 'a cyclophrenic', or 'and that belly like a navigation balloon – a clear example of meteorism, if not something worse' (p. 93–95). Dušnic expresses Johanides's view (similar to the Czech philosopher J.L. Fischer, or, not quite so traditional the Anglo-American Lewis Mumford's) that with mechanisation, humanity has been divorced from complete living, as experienced alienation of the soul.

'Everything is as wooden as the shelves of a new kitchen cabinet. Everywhere. Mass production: we live amongst practical people. Just think of the rush hour. Or, indeed, airports at midday. So, you find me, one single human being who is not dreaming non-stop about something.' He said slowly [...] and with a very sad voice.
'Even in the transfusion ward? Even theatre nurses?'
'All of them. Men and women. What do you expect of them? Clearly, you would be capable of asking a conductor to force a coloratura soprano to trill the word *zmrzlina*.'[8] (p. 8)

In the same vein is Dušnic's fear of art-collectors, whom he labels 'Europe's new ball bearings' (like investment bankers or

8   *zmrzlina* is Slovak for ice cream.

oligarchs). Finally, new in Johanides, and connected with the continuing eye theme are his frequent episodes concerning laughter. And it is again Dušnic who laughs most often. Thus he remarks. 'People laugh less and less. Isn't it terrible? After all, laughter cleans out the eyes. Like weeping.' (p. 8) In Dušnic's laughter Stefanides sees his friend's warmth, human understanding: 'He felt the power of Dušnic's merry, always mischievous kindness, his understanding kind-heartedness that is never tired by anything.' (pp. 6–7). Laughter also expresses Dušnic's selflessness: 'Then, however, he burst into an exuberant guffaw and continied in a decisive voice that excluded any shadow or sadness.' 'For sixty years I have been pretty sad, but today I'm perhaps saddest of all.' That contrasts completely with the consultant's laughter (which recalls Filip's laughter in *Najsmutnejšia oravská balada*) about which Stefanides speaks of his 'desire stronger than hunger to wash the consultant's laughter away' (p. 109).

Johanides's next book comprises two long short stories, *Zločin plachej lesbičky. Holomráz* (The Crime of a Shy Lesbian. Black Frost, 1991, title page, colophon date 1992, the last year of the existence of Czechoslovakia) and contains as much blood as his 1960s works and *Najsmutnejšia oravská balada*. Both stories are *Rahmenerzählungen* and the first has as its main framework a character, a psychiatrist Rudolf Tróger – and so we may see here some link with *Previesť cez most*. Both stories contain political murders; both portray a police state dominated by fear, and both have a Bulgarian connexion to *Zločin plachej lesbičky*, the character who dominates the action (but one not yet evidently the main character) looks forward to the post-prison Ostarok in *But Crime Does Punish*, for he had once been a lawyer and was now a senior officer of the criminal police, Jakub Dvojčák (dvojčák = double or even *Doppelgänger*). Dvojčák is one of Johanides's knowers; in this case he stops attending the regular canasta evenings with friends, for he always knows what cards the players have in their hands. It happens only twice, but he begins hard drinking when he 'knows'a death will soon take place in his proximity. On holiday in Bulgaria, he starts waking up every night at 1.30 a.m., and only after he hears the shot that kills a girl, as a professional, he realizes it was a planned attack and that the weapon had been a military revolver. After that he begins to sleep through the night. Soon, in a pub, he learns that the girl had been a lesbian. In the course of the story Dvojčák's wife apparently turns out to be a lesbian, her best friend, too, and the latter's daughter. In the end it appears probable that none of them is lesbian. The concept appears simply to be a synonym for anti-Communist. Then the girl shot at 1.30 a.m. is a political killing. A barman in the Bulgarian resort turns out to be a Bulgarian who had been trained by the Slovak secrect police. A story circulating in Czechoslovakia when Johanides was writing involved a Bulgarian honey trap frequently employed by Czechoslovak intelligence who left a trail of destruction from West Germany to the United Kingdom, to the USA. I never heard the ending of the story, but in Johanides's version related to me while he was writing *Zločin plachej lesbičky*, she was a clever, but infantile liar, and charmer – so difficult for the Communist intelligence services to control or to be sure the information she provided was reliable. Given the role of police homosexuals in *But Crime Does Punish*, and in real life, the importance a few homosexuals had in the control of intellectuals, Johanides is touching on Communism's invasion (sorry, special operations) of its citizens' intimate life. As we know, there is no evidence that Johanides had anything whatsoever against homosexuality, male or female. Dvojčák, who has a rich bourgeois family background and manners slightly prefigures the colonel in *But Crime Does Punish*. Dvojčák's character is summarized by the psychiatrist as follows: 'poor chap, immensely wretched – but a pure, honest fellow, a type that is probably beginning to die out in the world.' (p. 46) The main political content of *Holomráz* lies in consistent, strong criticism of anti-Gipsy racism. The main spy character here bears a common Gipsy name Dezső, in its Slovak (or Czech) version Dežo, actually half-Gipsy, perhaps too obviously the 'knower' of the story. The framework tells the story of a convulsive actor named Psotník (an old-fashioned word for a form of infantile convulsions) who moves into a village that appears to be inhabited only by high-ranking Party people. Psotník's neighbour Jabloncová, a fine Communist former prison worker who recorded in her notebook all the local goings on, and the conversations she witnesses. Her father was the Slovak who betrayed to the Germans the British intelligence officers who were all having a meeting together in one mountain hut during the Slovak National Uprising. The Germans surrounded the hut and set fire to it so that all the British agents were burnt alive. The account of this in the Public Records Office may have once disappeared; when I tried to get a copy at the time the Office had moved out of central London to Kew and dully became the The National Archive. Psotník becomes more and more aware of who is doing what in the village, from Jabloncová but mainly from Dežo and the village priest Piskač (literally whistler, fife-player but also colloquially referee), both of them warn him to go away. Dežo, the life affirmer, had lived through suffocating to death by copulation a Bucharest widow, who had been his great love. During the war Dežo had been in Auschwitz, but was saved from the gas chamber by his musicianship and ended up in a camp in western Poland. Here he witnessed further atrocities perpetrated against Russians and Bulgarians. After the war he married a Bulgarian woman and became a Communist Party local official, but was too honest to be able to endure his job. He was also the head of the local League of Anti-Fascist Fighters, and became so drunk when the League was celebrating the unveiling of a memorial to the Bulgarian partisans who had died in Slovakia that he fell down unconscious before the Bulgarian Ambassador in Prague and the consul in Bratislava. Soon after that he was sent to prison for murdering a salesgirl, who had actually been murdered by a local party boss's son Laco Gandža who persuades Dežo to take the blame so that all his sons secure good jobs. In *Holomráz* the reader will encounter a major point in Johanides's wisdom, in his constant exploring a moral and social preference for despising as against hating. If one hates, one shows no respect for an individual's dignity; if one despises, one is rejecting a person who neither has human dignity nor exhibits it; in summary, 'the incapacity to despise often offers a loophole for the entry of evil' (p. 73). *Holomráz* succeeds in its aim to be a distressing piece of literature.

In the same year, 1992, the last year of Czech-Slovak union, Johanides published a collection of three elegant short stories,

Krik drozdov pred spaním (Thrushes Screeching Before Sleep). The charwoman and lavatory cleaner of 'Autostrády potkanov' (Sewer-rat Motorways), Jozefína Haburová, is something of a gossip, but chiefly she is a sensitive woman who has been in a state of almost permanent shock since her father had given her such a violent strapping that her whole body was bleeding. The story itself proceeds from a conversation between Haburová and a senior civil servant Vjekár, who wants Haburová to stop talking to all and sundry about her discovery of the corpse of Jela Pletiarová; Vjekár initially claims to have been Jela's betrothed and states that if Haburová continues spreading the corpse story, he also is likely to be murdered. In Vjekár Johanides is talking about the 'dark secrets' that had been covered under so-called Communism; if uncovered in post-Communism will be met with violence of the same kind. The grandly elegant Jela had been going to the dogs before she was murdered. The title of the story emerges from Haburová's love of cats: one of the cats she feeds had been devoured by rats. Because of the proximity of a meat-canning factory (*cf.* the slaughterhouse in *Nie*) just underground there is a very motorway of sewer-rats. Rats are people like Vjekár and the people who, after Jela's murder, had broken into the undertaker's and set fire to the coffins (covering up truth). Haburová had been divorced by her engine-driver husband for a slip of a girl, but has a new sweetheart, the greengrocer Meerettich, and greengrocers are reputed to be strenuous gossips in Central Europe; Vjekár gets most of his information from Meerettich. The second piece in *Krik drozdov pred spaním,* 'Pamiatka Dona Giovanniho' (A Souvenir from Don Giovanni) constitutes a brief tale about a young opera singer who suddenly gets blood poisoning; the consultant in the accident and emergency ward tells him that his botulism will soon disappear, but he must not sing in *Don Giovanni* again. The reader does not learn whether the young man had been poisoned, indeed whether there is anything wrong with him. The consultant is working on intuition – which will save the singer. Johanides's statement on fate informs us how this insignificant episode fits in with the concealment theme of the collection:

Fate has been surprising from times immemorial: it has always something up its sleeve, stacks of coincidences, always in a different outfit, always differently masked. It always has been its principle to be an unexpected guest. But it has always tended to be one tone in common in all its words: the tone of the rat-catcher's pipe from the renowned ancient city of Hamelin. Fate addresses you using ancient works that might be likened to the action of a dream (p. 42).

The third piece in *Krik drozdov pred spaním*, 'Inzeráty pre večnosť' (Small-ads for eternity) takes us once more to the Shoah, indeed, it is more or less the title story, since the thrushes are those that sleep in the old trees that surround the mental hospital where the main character ends up. It is a tale of extreme violence, the framework of which is set during the rein of Nikita Khrushchev. The narrator is an apprentice journalist on the Slovak Communist daily, *Pravda*, who meets the elderly Múčenka. Múčenka is another 'knower'; in a restaurant he suddenly tells the journalist that one of the two men sitting at the next table will kill the other; he can tell from his eyes. He had seen such eyes before when, after his Jewish employer, Berger, had become bankrupt and sent him to work for a cousin in Lemberg (Leopol; setting is pre-First World War Lemberg; after the war Lwów and after the German-Soviet splitting of Poland and the post-war Western Allies' virtual recognition of the Nazi-Polish Fascist-Soviet agreement, Lviv). Múčenka's mother had been Jewish and died in childbed and his father had been Lutheran. In Lemberg Múčenka had fallen in love with a baroness who was a regular in the restaurant where he was a waiter. His new boss warns him that she had murdered her own children, and had been acquitted on trial because the chief witness, a manservant, had gone mad and killed himself. He tries to fall out of love and in despair, one day deliberately scalds her, and he sees this killer look in her eyes before she shoots him, luckily only in the hand. He has to leave Lemberg; in Petrograd he witnesses the Reds' mowing down two hundred noble schoolgirls coming over a bridge. In the Reds he sees the same look. He goes next to Berlin, and then Vienna, which he leaves after the *Anschluß* – and returns at last to Bratislava. Here he becomes promiscuous, endeavouring to find love by means of copulation, and one day, he goes to bed with a German woman who reminds him of the baroness; she notices his circumcision after their love-making, reports him to the authorities and he ends up in a concentration camp. We then encounter the killer look just after the liberation of concentration camps when an emaciated Jew notices in a Katowice market and approaches the athletic Jewish butcher who is selling food only to Jews and these Jews have to pay with a snippet of concentration-camp uniform or just a button. The emaciated Jew wants just a kosher sausage, but he is so horrified that the butcher's products are all being wrapped in pages from the Hebrew Book of Job (labelled by the butcher in a Jewish advertisement [*inzerát*] for eternity). The emaciated man now assumes the killer look, fishes out a pistol and shoots the butcher. In Johanides's next work, the brief novel *Kocúr a zimný človek* (A Tom-cat and a winter man, 1994) the action is set on Christmas Eve in 1992, the seventieth birthday of the wise Skielco (= a small piece of glass) who lives alone with his cat in his tower-block flat, well-stocked with all manner of hard alcohol. Skielco tries to drink in moderation, and his cat is a minor precursor of Ostarok's Regent, for the cat goes over to sit by the bottles when it decides its master has had enough. Skielco had fought with the Czechoslovak soldiers at Monte Cassino; been captured by the Germans and sent to Mauthausen (refrain of so many Johanides's stories). Thereafter he had loathed all Austrian Germans, for they had never done anything for the camp inmates. In this brief work Johanides displays a satirical picture of the complex racism that bubbles under the surface of modern Slovak society. A Vietnamese woman (nicknamed Lukriša, *i.e.* Lucretia) is badly injured in a traffic accident; she needs a blood transfusion, but the hospital has none of her group, whereupon a Gipsy member of the plaster-cast making unit offers his blood, and the doctors give her some of his blood. When she learns this and the medics tell her she should thank him, she finds the Gipsy, spits into his eyes, and screams that she did not need Gipsy blood. She claimed that if she'd known they would be giving her Gipsy blood she would have said she would rather kick the bucket on the spot. Another woman, one of three squabblers in Skielco's block, Rena, at first appears to be just another nasty selfish human being. In fact, in Rena, Johanides manifests his feminism in full throat. Rena represents the lot of women altogether, women tormented by the male from teenage onwards; one might see in the following mere hyperbole, but now-adays pictures of women with such lots, are commonplace, but not at all normal in Johanides's lifetime. Johanides was no prophet, but an uncommonly sensitive human being. Rena's life is one of frustration and the uncontrolled humiliation that she believes is woman's duty to accept/perform:

> She often experienced Sunday mornings at the end of autumn with its background of grey dawning as echoes of nocturnal insult; males were constantly insulting her body [...] she aired the flat when a lover departed and simultaneously watered the flowers and constructed a tridirectional draught. She loathed this confusion of fumes: the stench of beer, the radicle of male semen dried off in her knickers, the stench of socks full of the first, fresh, sated sweat drawn-down from the well-washed feet, the stench from male mouths caused by a damaged digestive tract, emerging from amongst fine well-cared-for teeth, which had completed their gnawing at Rena. She was not satisfied with this importunate, intrusive scents that acted on her like exciting decay, did not disperse in the surging of fresh, clean, indifferent air. She experienced the tiredness arising from a feelingless nocturnal – always vain, always numbing – gymnastics without massage, and she was incapable of crying. (*Kocúr a zimný človek*, 1994, p. 35)

In general in *Kocúr a zimný človek*, the minor figures, the cold teenage boys who kill the kittens, the women who would (with those gazes in their eyes that come from low pay and years of humiliation) all serve to draw a picture of the all too human inhumanity of tower-block society, under whichever ideology, Soviet socialist or market economy pseudo-democracy.

Johanides wrote another half-dozen books of fiction after *But Crime Does Punish* but they do not concern us here, for it stands to reason that they did not form any basis to the thinking behind the novel translated here. I shall, however, return to the main text and to two parallel scenes that make for a fine example that a literary text can take on new meanings over the years, of how a great literary work may change its meaning(s) without the reader having in any way to distort the author's original purposes.

To end, I take two parallel passages in *But Crime Does Punish* that express the two chief features Johanides sees smashing apart through human society. The first scene is that where a girl Ostarok takes out drinking and dancing not long after he is out of prison. The first, unnamed girl (anonymous because empty) has become drunk and sexually excited enough to demand coitus with Ostarok; he informs her of his balllessness; she registers the fact visually and then howls at Ostarok that he had no right to take her out if he was about to deprive her of the human right to coitus. Thus a picture of what the author frequently labels sexual cynicism/materialism. More important, it is also a picture of the general failure of Western democracy, not only in the formerly Communist land but at least since the 1970s everywhere, it has become universal that democracy has lost one its fundamental criteria that every right brings with it duties. Right without duties has nothing to do with democracy. Giving is disappearing from a world, where taking is praised over giving. Johanides is an exceptional writer because of the combination of a practical knowledge of duty and a suspicion of rights, his personal kindness and his concentrated failure to fall in with the compromise of most of his fellow Slovak writers. Students of the post-war Soviet bloc almost always forget that a large number of its citizens had direct contact with the brutality of the Soviet Communist Party and its satellites' extensions. Furthermore, Czechoslovakia was one of the few Soviet-led states in the bloc not to have a Red Army occupation force on its soil during the first twenty or so years after the Second World War. It was repeated over and over again that the Russians trusted the Czechs to maintain a Soviet-style regime, first because they had shown only loyalty, second, because they were capable of keeping the more rebellious Slovaks in order. Johanides's view on the Soviet or Russian party, whether it proclaimed socialism or nationalism is evident in the second episode that followed an evening in the pub. Here the girl is named Eva (not only the prime-woman and prime-mother, but also, conventionally, a name meaning life), perhaps to render the author's point of view indisputable. In this episode, you will remember, two secret policemen follow Ostarok, Eva and the future farmacist informer? secret policemen? Vrtiak. Eva shouts at the policemen as if to force them to admit that they were responsible. One of the policemen kicks Eva in the spleen to make sure she would die and the two of them run off. Anyway, the secret police have killed the prime-woman, the first person who knows about sexual pleasure as Eva, the representative of Life. Eva's death is the death of love, and the impact of Soviet-led party rule.

Gosfield, Essex, May 2022

ABOUT THE TRANSLATORS

Julia Sherwood is a translator from Slovak, Czech, Polish, Russian and German into English (with Peter Sherwood), as well as into Slovak. She was born and grew up in Bratislava, Czechoslovakia (now the Slovak Republic), but studied English and Slavonic languages and literature in Cologne, London and Munich. She is editor-at-large for Slovakia for *Asymptote*, and co-curates the website SlovakLiterature.Com. She lives in London. Her joint translations of with Peter Sherwood include Daniela Kapitáňová's *Samko Tále's Cemetery Book,* Pavel Vilikovský's *Fleeting Snow*, as well as books by Uršuľa Kovalyk, Balla and Ivana Dobrakovová, and from the Czech, *Freshta* by Petra Procházková and *Hana* by Alena Mornštajnová.

Peter Sherwood is a translator and scholar. He taught Hungarian at the School of Slavonic and East European Studies, University College London, from 1972 to 2007. From 2008 until his retirement in 2014 he was László Birinyi, Sr., Distinguished Professor of Hungarian Language and Culture at the University of North Carolina at Chapel Hill. In 2020 he won the Árpád Tóth Prize for Translation. His translations from the Hungarian include collections of essays by Béla Hamvas and Antal Szerb and, most recently, Ádám Bodor's novel *The Birds of Verhovina*. He lives in London.

MODERN SLOVAK CLASSICS

Published titles
Ján Johanides: *But Crime Does Punish*

Forthcoming
Ján Rozner: *Sedem dní do pohrebu*